James Bowie Middle School
700 Plantation Drive
Richmond, TX 77406

D1763061

JUNIOR DRUG AWARENESS

Marijuana

JUNIOR DRUG AWARENESS

Alcohol

Amphetamines and Other Stimulants

Cocaine and Crack

Diet Pills

Ecstasy and Other Club Drugs

Heroin

How to Say No to Drugs

Inhalants and Solvents

Marijuana

Nicotine

Over-the-Counter Drugs

Prozac and Other Antidepressants

Steroids and Other Performance-Enhancing Drugs

Vicodin, OxyContin, and Other Pain Relievers

JUNIOR DRUG AWARENESS

Marijuana

W. Scott Ingram

Junior Drug Awareness: Marijuana

Copyright © 2008 by Infobase Publishing

All rights reserved. No part of this book may be reproduced or utilized in any form or by any means, electronic or mechanical, including photocopying, recording, or by any information storage or retrieval systems, without permission in writing from the publisher. For information contact:

Chelsea House
An imprint of Infobase Publishing
132 West 31st Street
New York NY 10001

Library of Congress Cataloging-in-Publication Data

Ingram, Scott.
  Marijuana / W. Scott Ingram.
     p. cm. — (Junior drug awareness)
  Includes bibliographical references and index.
  ISBN 978-0-7910-9695-6 (hardcover)
  1. Marijuana—Juvenile literature. 2. Marijuana abuse—Juvenile literature. I. Title. II. Series.

  RC568.C2I44 2008
  616.86'35—dc22   2007024826

Chelsea House books are available at special discounts when purchased in bulk quantities for businesses, associations, institutions, or sales promotions. Please call our Special Sales Department in New York at (212) 967-8800 or (800) 322-8755.

You can find Chelsea House on the World Wide Web
at http://www.chelseahouse.com

Text design by Erik Lindstrom
Cover design by Jooyoung An

Printed in The United States of America

Bang NMSG 10 9 8 7 6 5 4 3 2 1

This book is printed on acid-free paper.

All links and web addresses were checked and verified to be correct at the time of publication. Because of the dynamic nature of the web, some addresses and links may have changed since publication and may no longer be valid.

CONTENTS

INTRODUCTION
Battling a Pandemic: A History of Drugs
in the United States   6
**by Ronald J. Brogan,
Regional Director of D.A.R.E. America**

1	**Marijuana: Read All About It**	12
2	**Marijuana Messages**	24
3	**Marijuana From Past to Present**	34
4	**What Marijuana Does to the Body**	56
5	**What Marijuana Does to the Mind**	69
6	**Getting Help**	81
	Chronology	95
	Glossary	97
	Bibliography	99
	Further Reading	103
	Photo Credits	105
	Index	106
	About the Authors	110

INTRODUCTION

Battling a Pandemic: A History of Drugs in the United States

When Johnny came marching home again after the Civil War, he probably wasn't marching in a very straight line. This is because Johnny, like 400,000 of his fellow drug-addled soldiers, was addicted to morphine. With the advent of morphine and the invention of the hypodermic needle, drug addiction became a prominent problem during the nineteenth century. It was the first time such widespread drug dependence was documented in history.

Things didn't get much better in the later decades of the nineteenth century. Cocaine and opiates were used as over-the-counter "medicines." Of course, the most famous was Coca-Cola, which actually did contain cocaine in its early days.

After the turn of the twentieth century, drug abuse was spiraling out of control, and the United States government stepped in with the first regulatory controls. In 1906, the Pure Food and Drug Act became a law. It required the labeling of product ingredients. Next came the Harrison Narcotics Tax Act of 1914, which outlawed illegal importation or distribution of cocaine and opiates. During this time, neither the medical community nor the general population was aware of the principles of addiction.

After the passage of the Harrison Act, drug addiction was not a major issue in the United States until the 1960s, when drug abuse became a much bigger social problem. During this time, the federal government's drug enforcement agencies were found to be ineffective. Organizations often worked against one another, causing counterproductive effects. By 1973, things had gotten so bad that President Richard Nixon, by executive order, created the Drug Enforcement Administration (DEA), which became the lead agency in all federal narcotics investigations. It continues in that role to this day. The effectiveness of enforcement and the so-called "Drug War" are open to debate. Cocaine use has been reduced by 75% since its peak in 1985. However, its replacement might be methamphetamine (speed, crank, crystal), which is arguably more dangerous and is now plaguing the country. Also, illicit drugs tend to be cyclical, with various drugs, such as LSD, appearing, disappearing, and then reappearing again. It is probably closest to the truth to say that a war on drugs can never be won, just managed.

Fighting drugs involves a three-pronged battle. Enforcement is one prong. Education and prevention is the second. Treatment is the third.

Although pandemics of drug abuse have been with us for more than 150 years, education and prevention were not seriously considered until the 1970s. In 1982, former First Lady Betty Ford made drug treatment socially acceptable with the opening of the Betty Ford Center. This followed her own battle with addiction. Other treatment centers—including Hazelton, Fair Oaks, and Smithers (now called the Addiction Institute of New York)—added to the growing number of clinics, and soon detox facilities were in almost every city. The cost of a single day in one of these facilities is often more than $1,000, and the effectiveness of treatment centers is often debated. To this day, there is little regulation over who can practice counseling.

It soon became apparent that the most effective way to deal with the drug problem was prevention by education. By some estimates, the overall cost of drug abuse to society exceeds $250 billion per year; preventive education is certainly the most cost-effective way to deal with the problem. Drug education can save people from misery, pain, and ultimately even jail time or death. In the early 1980s, First Lady Nancy Reagan started the "Just Say No" program. Although many scoffed at the program, its promotion of total abstinence from drugs has been effective with many adolescents. In the late 1980s, drug education was not science based, and people essentially were throwing mud at the wall to see what would stick. Motivations of all types spawned hundreds, if not thousands, of drug-education programs. Promoters of some programs used whatever political clout they could muster to get on various government agencies' lists of most effective programs. The bottom line, however, is that prevention is very difficult to quantify. It's nearly impossible to prove that drug use would have occurred if it were not prevented from happening.

Battling a Pandemic: A History of Drugs in the United States

In 1983, the Los Angeles Unified School District, in conjunction with the Los Angeles Police Department, started what was considered at that time to be the gold standard of school-based drug education programs. The program was called Drug Abuse Resistance Education, otherwise known as D.A.R.E. The program called for specially trained police officers to deliver drug-education programs in schools. This was an era in which community-oriented policing was all the rage. The logic was that kids would give street credibility to a police officer who spoke to them about drugs. The popularity of the program was unprecedented. It spread all across the country and around the world. Ultimately, 80% of American school districts would utilize the program. Parents, police officers, and kids all loved it. Unexpectedly, a special bond was formed between the kids who took the program and the police officers who ran it. Even in adulthood, many kids remember the name of their D.A.R.E. officer.

By 1991, national drug use had been halved. In any other medical-oriented field, this figure would be astonishing. The number of people in the United States using drugs went from about 25 million in the early 1980s to 11 million in 1991. All three prongs of the battle against drugs vied for government dollars, with each prong claiming credit for the reduction in drug use. There is no doubt that each contributed to the decline in drug use, but most people agreed that preventing drug abuse before it started had proved to be the most effective strategy. The National Institute on Drug Abuse (NIDA), which was established in 1974, defines its mandate in this way: "NIDA's mission is to lead the Nation in bringing the power of science to bear on drug abuse and addiction." NIDA leaders were the experts in prevention and treatment, and they had enormous resources. In

1986, the nonprofit Partnership for a Drug-Free America was founded. The organization defined its mission as, "Putting to use all major media outlets, including TV, radio, print advertisements and the Internet, along with the pro bono work of the country's best advertising agencies." The Partnership for a Drug-Free America is responsible for the popular campaign that compared "your brain on drugs" to fried eggs.

The American drug problem was front-page news for years up until 1990–1991. Then the Gulf War took over the news, and drugs never again regained the headlines. Most likely, this lack of media coverage has led to some peaks and valleys in the number of people using drugs, but there has not been a return to anything near the high percentage of use recorded in 1985. According to the University of Michigan's 2006 Monitoring the Future study, which measured adolescent drug use, there were 840,000 fewer American kids using drugs in 2006 than in 2001. This represents a 23% reduction in drug use. With the exception of prescription drugs, drug use continues to decline.

In 2000, the Robert Wood Johnson Foundation recognized that the D.A.R.E. Program, with its tens of thousands of trained police officers, had the top state-of-the-art delivery system of drug education in the world. The foundation dedicated $15 million to develop a cutting-edge prevention curriculum to be delivered by D.A.R.E. The new D.A.R.E. program incorporates the latest in prevention and education, including high-tech, interactive, and decision-model-based approaches. D.A.R.E. officers are trained as "coaches" who support kids as they practice research-based refusal strategies in high-stakes peer-pressure environments. Through stunning magnetic resonance imaging (MRI) images, students get to see tangible proof of how various substances diminish brain activity.

Will this program be the solution to the drug problem in the United States? By itself, probably not. It is simply an integral part of a larger equation that everyone involved hopes will prevent kids from ever starting to use drugs. The equation also requires guidance in the home, without which no program can be effective.

Ronald J. Brogan
Regional Director
D.A.R.E America

1

Marijuana: Read All About It

Studies done by the U.S. National Institutes of Health (NIH) estimate that more than 95 million Americans—about 40% of the population—have used marijuana. That makes marijuana the most widely used illegal drug in the United States. Yet, the story of marijuana is one of the most unusual stories of any illegal drug used in the United States today.

Of course, Americans use many drugs both legally and illegally. But marijuana is a drug that is in a special category. It does not have a long history of use in the United States as a drug, like tobacco or alcohol does. It is not processed from a plant into a powder, like heroin or cocaine. It is not manufactured with dangerous chemicals in illegal factories like methamphetamine. It is not considered **addictive** in the same way that these other

Distinctive leaves make the marijuana plant (*Cannabis sativa*) easy to recognize. The green, spiky leaves have become symbols of the drug.

illegal drugs—or even legal prescription drugs—are considered addictive. Using marijuana, however, can still be dangerous, and penalties for its use can be harsh.

A CLOSER LOOK AT MARIJUANA

The scientific name for marijuana is **Cannabis sativa**. Cannabis is an annual plant. That means it dies when cold weather arrives each year. It grows best in warm, sunny climates, and can reach 15 feet (nearly 5 meters) in height. The most recognizable parts of this plant are its leaves. Images of green, spiky marijuana leaves appear on everything from bumper stickers and T-shirts to drug use–prevention material. The leaves spread from a single point on a stem, like fingers from a person's hand. In most cases, a full-grown marijuana plant has leaves with between five and seven "fingers."

One of the most peculiar things about marijuana is that people don't always call it by that name. Few call it *sativa*, either. Most people use nicknames for it. Of course, other drugs have nicknames too, but few drugs have as many as marijuana. Most people call it pot, but it's also known as grass, reefer, weed, chronic, ganja, herb, skunk sinsemilla, mary jane, and mj, among other names.

In late summer, the plant's small, white flowers are in bloom. The drug marijuana is made from the dried flower buds and leaves of the *Cannabis sativa* plant. Some people also use a stronger form of marijuana, called **hashish**, which is made from the plant sap found inside the top leaves of the plant. "Hash" is dried and pressed into cookie-like sheets that are broken apart and smoked in pipes. Marijuana is most often smoked in cigarette or cigar form, or in pipes or pipe-like, water-filled devices called bongs. Marijuana can also be mixed with food and eaten.

The dried flower buds and leaves of the marijuana plant are used in preparing the drug, which is commonly smoked.

THE CANNABINOIDS

A marijuana plant contains more than 400 chemicals. About 60 of these chemicals belong to a group called **cannabinoids**. The cannabinoid that has the greatest effect on humans has a very long name: delta-9-tetrahydrocannabinol. It is most often called **THC**, from three letters in **t**etra**h**ydro**c**annabinol; the higher the percentage of THC in marijuana, the greater its effect on the brain. In the 1970s and 1980s, scientific research measured the average THC level of marijuana in the United States at about 3.5%. In recent years, however, THC percentages have increased. According to the Marijuana Potency Project at the University of Mississippi, the average level of THC in marijuana rose to about 7% in 2003. By 2006, it had risen to about 8.5%.

The strength of marijuana depends on where it is grown and when it is harvested, but female plants usually have a higher percentage of THC than male plants. Male plants are usually taller than female plants. They have thicker stems and fewer branches and leaves than female plants. In a natural setting, male plants produce pollen that pollinates the female plant. Once the female plant is pollinated, seeds are produced. Female plants can produce THC without pollination. These plants are known as *sinsemilla*—Spanish for "without seeds."

Some of the strongest marijuana has THC levels of about 15%. According to the Marijuana Potency Project report released in April 2007, the highest THC concentration found in marijuana was 33.12%, found in a sample from Oregon.

When a person smokes a marijuana cigarette or takes marijuana in some other form, THC and other chemicals enter the user's body. They travel from the lungs to the bloodstream. From there, the THC reaches the brain

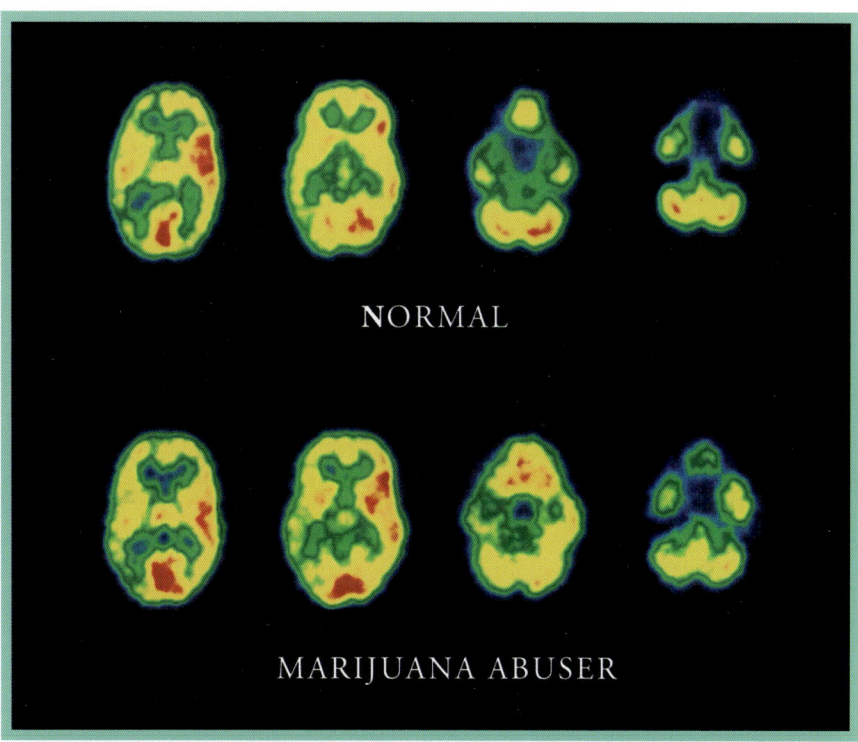

The brains of a marijuana user (*bottom*) and a non-user (*top*) are compared in these colored positron emission tomography (PET) scans. Marijuana contains the psychoactive drug tetrahydrocannabinol (THC), which reduces brain activity in the cerebellum. These scans show the cerebellum to be the lower parts of the scans. The drug-free brain scan shows the cerebellum with more red areas, indicating high brain activity. The drug user's scans show fewer red areas over time because marijuana usage causes a lack of coordination and poor spatial judgment.

and then the rest of the body. Smoking is the fastest way for THC to enter the bloodstream. It is absorbed by lung tissue in seconds. People who smoke usually feel its effect within a few minutes. The effect becomes strongest between 10 to 30 minutes after smoking, and generally wears off within 2 to 3 hours.

When people eat marijuana, THC enters the stomach, where the blood absorbs it. From the stomach, blood carries THC to the rest of the body. When marijuana is eaten, the high takes longer to occur, but its effects last much longer: People who eat marijuana usually feel the effects between 30 to 60 minutes after eating it, but the effects but can last up to 6 hours.

WHY DO PEOPLE USE MARIJUANA?

Most often, people smoke marijuana for the feelings that occur when the THC interacts with the brain. Marijuana smokers use terms such as "high," "buzzed," or "stoned" to describe the sensation that occurs. Users often say that they feel carefree and happy at first, and then they feel relaxed, and sometimes sleepy. Marijuana users also report an increased sense of sight, sound, and taste. In most cases, these feelings are pleasant, and most marijuana users say they use the drug to relax.

Some people use marijuana for medical reasons. Medical marijauna use will be covered in depth in later chapters. In general, doctors in states that permit medical marijuana use will prescribe it to their patients to relieve pain, nausea, and vomiting from cancer treatments; to relieve sleeplessness, migraine headaches, and/or depression; and to ease pain from an eye disorder known as glaucoma.

WHO SMOKES MARIJUANA?

One unusual part of the story of marijuana in the United States is the way its use spread throughout U.S. society. Today, millions of Americans use this illegal drug. But marijuana was almost unknown as an intoxicating drug in the United States until the early twentieth century, according to research done by Charles Whitebread, a law professor at the University

WHAT IS HEMP?

One name that is sometimes substituted for marijuana is **hemp**. Although the two names are used as synonyms, hemp is actually a very different kind of cannabis that has far lower levels of cannabinoids than marijuana smoked by users today. A person would have to smoke extremely large amounts of hemp in order to feel anything.

Hemp has uses that do not involve drug use. Fiber from the tough, stringy plant stalk is used to make rope, cloth, paper, cardboard, and fiberboard. Hemp cloth resembles linen, and many people consider it better than cotton for making clothing. Paper made from hemp is considered by many people to be better than paper made from trees. Papermaking using hemp requires less land for trees and results in less pollution.

Hemp was once widely grown in the United States, and its fiber was used to make rope, as well as canvas for ship sails. In fact, the word *canvas* comes from the word *cannabis*. It has many other uses, too. At one time, oil from hemp plants was used in oil lamps. Some scientists today say that hemp oil could be used instead of petroleum products in industry because it is easy to produce and gives off less pollution. Hemp oil pressed from the stalk is used in paint and varnish. Hemp seed is a nutritious seed that is used in birdseed, and also in certain breakfast cereals.

Today, some people believe that hemp should be grown more widely in the United States for fiber, fuel, and other uses. Owning hemp products, such as hemp rope or a

(continues on page 20)

(continued from page 19)

A store called Botany Bay in Richmond, Kentucky, sells products made from hemp. These products include hats, backpacks, lotion, shampoo, books, and writing paper.

hemp shirt, is legal. However, under federal law, it is illegal to grow or possess cannabis in any plant form, including hemp, in the United States.

of Southern California. Whitebread's research found that the use of marijuana as a drug in the United States began with the arrival of Mexican immigrants to the United States in the early twentieth century. (The word *marijuana* is the Mexican Spanish term immigrants used for the drug.) Until 1937, there were no federal laws against smoking marijuana. But during a period of about 50 years, the use of marijuana spread from the southwestern United States to cities in the Midwest, the East, and beyond.

The population that used marijuana became larger in the 1960s, a time of great social and cultural change in the United States. The largest part of the population during that time was made up of young people known as "baby boomers." These people were born from 1946 to 1964. Many baby boomers rejected the conservative attitudes of their parents and other adults. One way in which they rebelled was by using marijuana.

From the mid 1960s to the late 1970s, marijuana use spread across U.S. society, mainly due to these baby boomers. In 1965, for example, only 1.8% of young people ages 18 to 25 had ever used marijuana. Beginning in 1967, use increased until 1979 when it reached about 20%. By 1982, people in that age group who used marijuana had increased to about 55%. In other words, what in the early 1900s was a drug used mainly by immigrants became a drug used by Americans of all social groups by the end of the century. And its use was most common among young people between the ages of 18 and 25.

The spread of marijuana use to mainstream America explains why millions of Americans say they have used marijuana in their lifetime. Many baby boomers who took part in the spread of marijuana use in the 1960s are now middle aged and have not used marijuana for many years. Some presidential candidates and former presidents have acknowledged using marijuana as college students, as have congressmen and high-ranking members of the federal judicial system.

What makes marijuana unique among drugs in the United States is its use across generations in every part of society. It is an illicit, or illegal, drug in the same category as heroin or cocaine. But relatively few people use those drugs, whereas ten of millions have tried marijuana or use it regularly. Studies by the National Institute on Drug Abuse (NIDA) show that the average user today is between the ages of 18 and 30; the average age of first

THE NATION'S LARGEST CASH CROP

One way to understand how widely marijuana has spread through U.S. society is to measure how much of the drug is grown and sold in the United States. In other words, what is its value as a **cash crop**? A cash crop is a plant product sold for money. Many people might think that the nation's largest cash crops would be corn or wheat. But in December

Indiana state police and U.S. Drug Enforcement Administration agents take control of a field of marijuana plants in LaPorte County, Indiana, in 2005. Indiana officials said it was one of the largest cultivated marijuana drug busts in the state.

use is 17. More men than women are regular users. Men are also more likely to have smoked marijuana over the course of their lives.

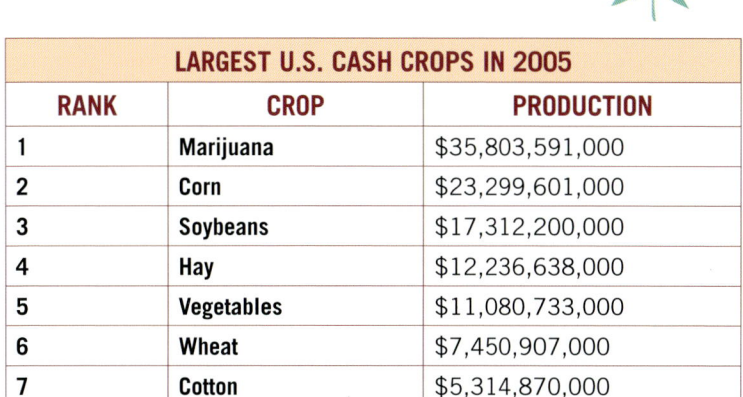

LARGEST U.S. CASH CROPS IN 2005		
RANK	CROP	PRODUCTION
1	Marijuana	$35,803,591,000
2	Corn	$23,299,601,000
3	Soybeans	$17,312,200,000
4	Hay	$12,236,638,000
5	Vegetables	$11,080,733,000
6	Wheat	$7,450,907,000
7	Cotton	$5,314,870,000

2006, the research group DrugScience.org released figures that showed marijuana was the nation's largest cash crop.

The DrugScience.org report claimed that the value of marijuana grown in the United States is more than $35 billion. That is more than the value of such legal cash crops as corn, soybeans, and wheat. The study also showed that marijuana was the top cash crop in 12 states and among the top three cash crops in 30 states.

The state with the largest marijuana harvest is California. It is estimated that about $13.8 billion of marijuana was grown there in 2005. That is a dollar amount greater than state's grapes, vegetables, and hay combined.

2

Marijuana Messages

In the 1930s, most Americans believed that marijuana was one of the most dangerous drugs ever to enter the United States. But that fear only lasted until young people in the 1960s discovered that some of the reported dangers of marijuana might be exaggerated.

Most people can probably list many reasons why smoking marijuana is a bad idea. Yet, despite this knowledge, people still use it. Health professionals face difficulties when trying to convince young people that using marijuana is not a smart decision. Some people believe if use of marijuana is so widespread, it may not be very harmful. Just because marijuana is one of the most commonly used drugs, however, does not mean it is without risks.

RISKY CHOICE

Smoking marijuana is a risky choice that can cause emotional, social, and legal problems. One large organization that works to get this message across about marijuana and other drugs is the National Institute on Drug Abuse (NIDA). NIDA is part of the National Institutes of Health, one of the largest agencies in the U.S. government. In recent years, NIDA has found evidence that the anti-marijuana message is reaching young people.

How do NIDA researchers know that young people get the message? Simple: They ask. For more than 20 years, NIDA has asked young people about drug and alcohol use. Every year, NIDA surveys students in the eighth, tenth, and twelfth grades—almost 50,000 students in more than 400 schools—across the United States. Young people who take the NIDA survey do not use their names. That way they can truthfully answer questions without fear of punishment if they admit that they have used drugs or alcohol.

FEWER TEENS ARE TRYING IT

One of the first questions the NIDA survey asks is whether a student has used marijuana in the past month. In 2006, the survey showed that in all three grades, the number of students who said they had smoked marijuana in the past month had dropped, compared to the results of the 2005 survey. Furthermore, the number of teenagers in all three grades who said they had smoked pot in the past month had been dropping steadily since 2001. In 2001, an average of about 17% of students in all three grades said they had smoked marijuana in the past month. In 2006, an average of about 13% answered yes to that survey question.

The same NIDA survey also asked students in all three grades whether they had smoked marijuana in the past year. Again, there was positive news in the 2006 survey. The number of young people who said they had smoked marijuana in the past year fell in all three grades. Dr. Nora Volkow, the director of NIDA, summed up the results of this finding: "Past-year use of marijuana has fallen by 36% among eighth graders, 28% among tenth graders, and 18% among twelfth graders since the peak abuse years in the 1990s. This is great news."

SUMMERTIME DRUG ABUSE

Most kids can't wait to get out of school for summer vacation. No more teachers. No more books. Nothing to do but hang out and . . . smoke marijuana? In some cases, that's the truth. According to the White House Office of National Drug Control Policy, summer is the time of year when young people are more likely to try marijuana for the first time.

A study by the National Drug Control Policy Office shows that first-time marijuana use increases 40% during June and July. Each day, according to the study, about 6,300 young people try marijuana for the first time. Researchers believe that the increase in new marijuana users during the summer occurs for two main reasons: There are often no adults around, and children have a lot more free time. Research shows that unsupervised young people are four times more likely to use marijuana than those who are under adult supervision.

Another NIDA survey question asked young people whether they had ever used marijuana in their lives. Like the other questions, the results showed a sharp drop from previous years in all three age groups. The largest drop in lifetime use of marijuana was among eighth graders—and it was the largest drop since 1996. This means that fewer young people are making the decision to smoke marijuana early in adolescence. The steep drop among tenth graders was also good news. In 2005, about 34% of tenth graders said that they had smoked marijuana at some time. A year later, that percentage had fallen to about 31%.

These drops were encouraging, but the results of another question caused concern. That question asked whether marijuana was "easily" or "very easily" available in school or in the community. In other words, if a young person wanted to try marijuana, could he or she obtain it? The overwhelming answer, according to the NIDA survey, was *yes*. More than 70% of tenth graders who took the survey said they could easily or very easily obtain marijuana. NIDA now estimates that about 5 million people between 12 and 17 years old can buy marijuana in one hour or less. Another 5 million can buy marijuana within a day. But, as shown by the other survey questions, most students did not take that risk.

JOB NOT DONE

All of this might seem like positive news, but there is another way of looking at these statistics. For one, young people are still abusing illegal substances. Statistically, more teenagers smoke cigarettes and drink alcohol than smoke marijuana, although cigarettes and alcohol are both still illegal at certain ages. In addition, the NIDA survey shows that the number of tenth graders who have ever smoked marijuana dropped from about 34%

to about 31%. But that still means that about one out of every three teenagers has smoked marijuana at some time in his or her life.

A further look at the number of young people who have used marijuana shows that the "good news" may not be as good as it first appears. Although marijuana use in 2006 compared to past years fell in all three grades, the drop was not as steep among older students as it was among eighth graders. Simply put: As young people enter high school, the chances increase that they will smoke marijuana.

NIDA surveys back up the usage claims. In 2006, about 16% of eighth graders stated that they had used marijuana in their lifetime. As has been mentioned, that rose to 31% of tenth graders. By twelfth grade, about 42% of students said they had used marijuana. So, some students who said no to marijuana in middle school turned around and said yes in high school. "We know that the job is not yet done" in educating young people about marijuana, Volkow said.

Part of the job that Volkow defines as "not yet done" is convincing young people that smoking marijuana is risky. In 2005, about 19% of teenagers perceived a "great risk" in using marijuana, compared to about 16% in 1998. While it is good news that more young people see marijuana as a "great risk," a closer look shows that about four out of every five teenagers did *not* see that "great risk."

Another survey result also worries health professionals. Students in all three grades were asked whether regular use of marijuana was "harmful," meaning physically dangerous. Among eighth graders in the 2006 survey, more than 73% considered regular use of marijuana harmful. That percentage dropped to about 65% among tenth graders. It then dropped to 58% of twelfth graders.

The message is clear: As teenagers get older, they see less harm in regular use of marijuana. According to NIDA, each day about 6,000 people use marijuana for the first time—and two-thirds of the first-time users are younger than 18.

DO ADS WORK?

Between 1998 and 2004 NIDA spent about $1.4 billion on ads that attempted to convince teenagers to say no to marijuana. One ad showed young people getting high on marijuana and causing terrible accidents, such as running over a little girl on a bike. To judge whether the ads had any impact, NIDA hired a research company to survey how well the ads worked—or didn't work.

The research showed that, not only were the ads unsuccessful, but, they also actually seemed to increase the likelihood that some groups of young people would try marijuana. In fact, the more times young people saw the ads, the more likely they were to become curious about marijuana and to try it. Research showed that in areas where the ads were broadcast, the rates of first-time drug use actually increased among white males between 14 and 16 years old. In some ways, this is similar to what happened in the 1960s when young people were warned that marijuana was a "deadly poison" and became curious about the drug as a result.

WIDESPREAD USE, EVEN AMONG ADULTS

Of course, compared to teenagers who grew up in the peak years of marijuana use in the 1970s and early 1980s, young people today are much less likely to use marijuana. But now, the teenagers of the 1970s and 1980s are adults, and some still smoke marijuana. A 2006 article in the *Los Angeles Times* noted that "the market value of pot produced in the U.S. exceeds $35 billion—far more than the crop value of such important farm products such as corn, soybeans, and hay."

The large amount of marijuana grown in the United States isn't the only worry for health professionals. In early 2007, another *Los Angeles Times* article reported

WHY YOUNG PEOPLE SAY NO TO POT

The results of the 2006 NIDA survey show that the number of young people who have decided to stay away from marijuana increased from 2001 to 2006. NIDA wanted to learn more about possible reasons for this important news and to determine what kinds of ads might better target those who are uncertain about whether to try marijuana. And so, to learn more, the NIDA survey also asks young people *why* they have decided to say no.

Results from 2006 showed that about two-thirds of the teenagers ages 13 to 17 who don't smoke said that losing the respect of their family members and friends is the main reason they say no. Half of the young people who did not use marijuana said there was a "great risk" that they would lose important friendships if they smoked marijuana. Almost 70% of those who said no to marijuana said that they had *no* friends who used the drug. That number was up from 62% in 2002.

Specific reasons that were given for saying no were "getting in trouble with the law" or "losing a driver's license." Some young people pointed out that smoking marijuana could hurt their grades in school and perhaps prevent them

that the cost of supporting the military wars in Iraq and Afghanistan had led to a reduction in the amount of federal money available for the war on drugs. According to the article, since 2003 "the Pentagon has reduced by more than 62% its surveillance over Caribbean and

A colorful wall mural in New York City's Harlem neighborhood reminds young people to say no to drugs.

from getting into a good college. Other reasons were largely social: missing out on fun activities, acting stupidly or foolishly, being lonely, getting depressed, or becoming boring.

Pacific Ocean routes that are used to smuggle . . . marijuana. . . . At the same time, the Navy is deploying one-third fewer patrol boats in search of smugglers."

MARIJUANA'S FORGOTTEN COSTS

As mentioned, almost three out of four high school seniors feel that using marijuana regularly is not harmful to their health. So, if a young person feels that he is safe—if, for example, he sees adults smoking marijuana—he might think it's okay to smoke marijuana himself.

There is no solid evidence that marijuana acts as a **gateway drug** for everyone, leading smokers directly to hard drugs and life-threatening drug abuse. But if a person comes from a family with a background of **addiction**, marijuana could indeed serve as a gateway to other drugs. There is also some link between cigarette smoking and marijuana, but it is reversed: Tobacco use can open the gateway to marijuana.

People once claimed that marijuana could be as harmful as heroin or crack cocaine. Experts now agree, however, that exaggerating the dangers of marijuana has never worked in keeping people from it. What *is* true, though, is that using marijuana can cause more than social or legal problems.

There is one fact about marijuana on which all researchers agree: Smoking marijuana affects the brain. It can hurt a person's ability to think clearly and lead to risky decisions about other personal behavior. It can also cause short-term harm to memory. That is especially true for teenagers, whose brains are still developing. Like all parts of the body, some important areas of the brain are not fully grown in adolescence. That's not a scare tactic—it is information based on the most recent scientific research. To put it simply: Young people who smoke marijuana are taking risks that they may not understand because their brains are not fully able to understand what the drug is doing to them.

Many people—young and old—think that the main problem with marijuana is that it is illegal. In other words, they think the only harm that can come from using marijuana is punishment. For some young people, that is reason enough to stay away. Yet, none of the reasons given on the NIDA survey mentions *health* as a reason to say no to marijuana. All of the reasons come from the outside: friends' disapproval, family issues, legal troubles, and social problems.

Marijuana From Past to Present

Marijuana's history in the United States as a recreational drug is short compared to some other drugs. It has only become widely used in U.S. society since the mid-1960s. But in fact, cannabis has been grown in the United States since colonial times for use as hemp. The world history of cannabis, however, goes back much further than the 1600s. It has been used to make rope, cloth, and paper. It has also been used as medicine, as food, for religious ceremonies, and as an **intoxicant** since prehistoric times.

ANCIENT CHINA AND CANNABIS
Archeologists discovered the first recorded use of cannabis on the island nation of Taiwan, located off the coast of China. They discovered a prehistoric village site

Hemp was woven into fabric in ancient China. This image shows a religious scene done in silk embroidery on hemp cloth. It was created during the Tang dynasty in eighth century China.

there that was more than 10,000 years old. Among the artifacts they recovered were pieces of pottery that had been decorated by pressing strips of hemp cord into the wet clay before it hardened.

Written records from the Chinese Empire show that hemp use developed from simple cords into fabric. In 1972, a burial site from the Chou dynasty (1122–249 B.C.) was discovered. At the site were scraps of hemp cloth. Records preserved for thousands of years show that the ancient Chinese also used the strong fiber for shoes. Ancient writings have many passages that warn poor people to plant hemp so that they will have clothes. (Wealthy Chinese rulers usually wore silk clothes.)

As the Chinese became more familiar with hemp, farmers discovered that male plants produced a better fiber. On the other hand, the female plant produced the better seeds. The plant's seeds became an important food source for people in ancient China, along with rice and millet.

Interestingly, scientists and historians would not know of the uses of hemp in ancient China if the information had not been written down on another Chinese invention: paper. The Chinese made their paper by crushing hemp fibers and mulberry tree bark, and then placing the mixture in a tank of water. Fibers from the two plants would become tangled when mixed. When this paste was dried in molds, the fibers formed sheets that became writing paper. Archeologists have discovered fragments of paper containing hemp fiber in China that they have dated to the first century B.C.

CANNABIS AS MEDICINE

It makes sense that as cannabis became one of the most widely grown crops in China, its other properties would be discovered. By the first century A.D., the Chinese recognized cannabis for its uses in medicine. A text about herbs from that time describes the uses of *ma,* the Chinese word for cannabis. According to the text, *ma* was to be given in cases involving menstrual cramps, gout, rheumatism, malaria, constipation, and absentmindedness. By the second century A.D., ma was mixed with wine to form ma-yo. Ma-yo was used as a numbing agent during surgery.

EARLY INTOXICANT USE

The Chinese were the first people to use cannabis for food, clothes, paper, and medicine. Therefore, it is not surprising that they were also the first people to describe the physical effects of smoking marijuana, drinking it mixed in liquid, and eating it. In general, writing from ancient China strongly condemns the use of cannabis as an intoxicant. One text from the first century A.D. claimed that eating too many cannabis seeds caused people to "see demons." The text also claimed that taking cannabis over a long period of time enabled people to "communicate with the spirits."

CANNABIS IN INDIA

Cannabis was also common outside China. The earliest religious stories from India had references to cannabis, too. According to one story, the Hindu god Siva sat beneath the cool shade of a cannabis plant to escape the heat of the midday Sun. Curious about this plant he had never seen, Siva ate some leaves. He felt so energized that cannabis became his favorite food. Siva became known as the Lord of Bhang.

In ancient India, the term *bhang* was a name used for cannabis, but it did not mean only the plant itself.

A dancing Siva is shown on the Temple of Kailasanatha in Kanchipuram, Tamil Nadu, India. Stories about the Hindu god Siva often involve the cannabis plant.

It usually referred to a drink made with cannabis leaves, which was about as strong as the marijuana used in the United States today. The first reference to bhang's mind-altering effects appears in sacred texts of Hinduism called the Vedas, which were written between 2000 and 1400 B.C. One of these texts calls bhang one of the "herbs . . . which release us from anxiety."

CANNABIS MOVES WESTWARD

People from the Scythian culture of Central Asia were the first to bring cannabis to civilizations in the West. By that time, Asian cultures had used cannabis for food, clothing, medicine, and as an intoxicant for centuries. In about 700 B.C., people known as the Scythians migrated toward modern day Iran and further into Turkey and northern Greece. These people wore hemp clothing and used cannabis in other ways as well.

One of the most widely known descriptions of cannabis use in Western culture was in the writing of the famous Greek historian Herodotus. In the fifth century B.C., Herodotus described the funeral of a Scythian king. Warriors loyal to the king made animal sacrifices at his grave, Herodotus reported. They then sat in tents and dumped cannabis seeds onto stones heated in a fire. The seeds gave off smoke, which the warriors inhaled. According to Herodotus, this caused the Scythians to "howl with joy."

Cannabis continued to make its way toward Europe. Eventually, its uses were described by people of the greatest empire of that time: Rome. The Roman scientist Disocorides wrote about cannabis in a book about wild plants of the empire. He called cannabis a medicinal plant. Cannabis, wrote Disocorides, was more than just an important source of fiber for ropes. The oil from its seeds was helpful in treating earaches, he said. Similarly,

The ancient writings of Greek historian Herodotus (*above*) often included mentions of cannabis. While historians argue that his work is not completely accurate, Herodotus is the primary source for history from the fifth century, including the Greco-Persian Wars.

the Roman scientist Galen wrote that wealthy Romans ate a dessert made with marijuana seeds. Galen warned that although the dessert caused a pleasant sensation, eating too many seeds "affects the head by sending to it a warm and toxic vapor."

As ancient people migrated west from Asia, they carried cannabis seeds into Europe. In 1896, a German archaeologist uncovered a tomb that contained an urn filled with plant remains and cannabis seeds, which he dated to about 400 B.C. Like most ancient people, Europeans valued cannabis for its fibers to make rope and cloth, not as an intoxicant. The earliest use of hemp for ropes in France dates from about 200 B.C.; the French manufacture of hemp fabric is almost as old. Hemp ropes were also found in the ruins of a Roman fort in Great Britain, which was occupied between A.D. 140 and 180. Studies show that cannabis was first cultivated in England in about A.D. 400. Hemp ropes more that 1,500 years old have been found in Iceland as well, at several sites. Archeologists believe the seagoing Vikings were behind this, because their ships needed strong ropes for raising and lowering sails as they crossed the unknown waters of the North Atlantic. Scraps of cloth and fishing line made from hemp have also been found in Viking graves in Norway. In addition, cannabis seeds have been found in the remains of Viking ships that date back to A.D. 850.

CANNABIS AND EUROPEAN EXPLORATION

As archeologists have discovered, cannabis was an important plant to people of Western Europe by the beginning of the Middle Ages (approximately A.D. 500 to 1500). It was the Italians who first began large-scale cultivation of the plant. This occurred in the fourteenth and fifteenth centuries, a time that is now known as the

King Henry VIII of England issued a law requiring British farmers to grow hemp. The hemp was used to make sails and rope for ships.

age of exploration. Sailing vessels from Italy, Portugal, and eventually Spain began to make long sea voyages. The need for hemp ropes and hemp fabric for sails grew as nations pushed toward the "New World" of the Americas.

By the 1500s, the rulers of England realized that they needed hemp if their country wanted to send sailing vessels to the Americas. In 1533, King Henry VIII commanded that all farmers set aside a certain percentage of their land to grow hemp. Those who did not paid a fine.

CANNABIS IN THE ENGLISH COLONIES

The English settlers who founded the colony at Jamestown, Virginia, in 1607 did not cross the Atlantic to raise hemp. Like other Europeans, they came to the Americas in search of gold. But they found no gold in Virginia. Thus, in 1611, the royal governor of the colony informed the colonists that they were expected to grow hemp.

By 1616, colonist John Rolfe wrote that the colonists had raised hemp that was of better quality than that "in England or Holland." But a plant native to North America soon captured the interests of these first colonists: tobacco. Within a decade, the demand in Europe for American tobacco was enormous. As a crop, tobacco was easier to grow and harvest than hemp. It was also much more valuable. Colonists ignored the orders to grow hemp and instead tried to become wealthy by planting tobacco on all of the settlement's land.

HEMP IN NEW ENGLAND

Many of the settlers who landed at Plymouth, Massachusetts, in 1620 went there in search of religious freedom. But many others hoped to earn money through fishing or trade with Native Americans. Few of the Pilgrims, and few of the Puritans who arrived 10 years later in 1630, wanted to spend their time growing raw materials for England's merchants. Cannabis, however, was one of the first crops grown in the Massachusetts Bay Colony because hemp was needed in the colonies.

The shipbuilding industry in Salem, Massachusetts, was strong by 1635. That's when the town opened a workshop devoted to making rope out of the strongest material available: hemp.

In 1629, shipbuilding began in the village of Salem, Massachusetts. By 1635, the town's first ropewalk—a workshop for making hemp rope—had been established. Shipbuilders needed this rope, called rigging rope, to hoist sails. Rigging rope could be made from other plants, too, such as flax. But, as people in Asia had known for thousands of years, the best material for rope was hemp because of its strength and durability.

In 1640, the General Assembly of Connecticut feared that colonists there might die from the winter cold if they did not raise fiber-bearing crops such as hemp. The assembly asked colonists to raise hemp so that "we might in time have a supply of cloth among ourselves." The need for hemp became so great that the colonial assemblies in Massachusetts and Connecticut passed laws requiring every household to plant hemp seed.

HEMP AND THE AMERICAN REVOLUTION

By the time of the American Revolution in 1775, hemp was one of the most important crops in the British colonies. Some places such as Hemphill, Hempfield, and Hempstead took their name from the plant. Both George Washington and Thomas Jefferson grew cannabis along with tobacco on their plantations in Virginia. When the war heated up in 1776, colonists who did not fight raised raw materials to support the Patriot cause. One of the most important raw materials, after food crops such as wheat, was hemp.

In Virginia, more than 18 ropewalks were opened to make hemp fiber into rope to supply the colonial navy. Rope and sails (also made from hemp fiber) were so important that some colonial assemblies declared that any man who raised hemp or worked in a ropewalk for at least six months did not have to serve in the military.

Hemp, however, was more than just fiber for clothes, rope, and sails. It was used for money as well. Paper money had almost no value in the colonies. In Virginia, for example, it took about 1,000 of that colony's paper dollars to equal one dollar in silver. No one believed in the value of paper money at that time. Instead, the economy was run on the barter system: People traded items they had for items other people had. One trade item that had value for every colonist was hemp. It became the "money standard" for the first decade of the new United States.

CANNABIS IN THE SPANISH EMPIRE

The first cannabis that was brought to Mexico came with the conquistadors of Hernando Cortes's army in 1520. The hot climate in Mexico and the other parts of the Spanish Empire in the Americas was perfect for growing the plant. As they did in the case of extracting gold and other resources from the land, the Spaniards forced natives to do the hard work of harvesting hemp and removing the fibers from the stalk. Hemp became a successful business almost overnight. But in about 1550, the governor of New Spain (which included Mexico, parts of the United States, and Central America) declared that growth of the crop should be limited because the native people were using the leaves as intoxicants.

By the 1700s, Spain's economic problems forced the country to turn back to its colonial empire for raw materials. In 1777, experts in growing hemp came from Spain to various parts of New Spain. These experts taught farmers how to grow, harvest, and prepare hemp for market. Orders from the king instructed all colonial governors to demand that hemp be grown in New Spain. In Mexico, the rulers decided that the warm climate in the province of California was perfect for hemp farming.

The area around San Jose, in the northern part of what is now the state of California, was the first area to grow hemp, in 1801. In 1807, California produced about 13,000 pounds (about 6,000 kg) of hemp. Three years later, California produced more than 220,000 pounds (100,000 kg) of hemp. Almost half of the harvest came from Santa Barbara. Good harvests were also produced around San Jose, Los Angeles, and San Francisco.

CANNABIS AS AN INTOXICANT

Although hemp was one of the most important crops in world history for thousands of years, its use as a medicine or an intoxicant was not widely known in Europe at first. Some peasants in the Middle Ages and later eras used cannabis in those ways, but the majority of people in Europe, and those who grew cannabis in the Americas, valued it only because of its incredibly strong fibers.

Among Europeans, the main plant intoxicant was North American tobacco.

Over the centuries, European explorers and merchants sailed to Arab countries in the Middle East and to India, where the cannabis plant was used not only for fiber. Its leaves and resin were eaten, smoked, and made into drinks. In those regions, many people followed the Islamic faith, which prohibits the use of alcohol. As a result, cannabis in various forms became the most widely used intoxicant. Because of the great distance between Asia and Europe, however, that information was not common knowledge. In addition, Europeans already had their intoxicants of choice—alcohol and tobacco—and so they were not on the hunt for anything new.

It is believed that the first widespread smoking of marijuana and hashish—cannabis resin—in Europe began in the late 1700s. In 1798, French soldiers from Napoleon's army returned from Egypt. In that Muslim country, cannabis and its by-products were popular intoxicants. Many of the soldiers returned to France with these drugs.

CANNABIS IN NINETEENTH-CENTURY AMERICA

In the United States, the use of hemp fibers for rope and sails declined in the 1800s for several reasons. First, the age of sailing vessels came to an end with the development of steam power. Fewer ropes and sails were needed because ships were powered by steam. In addition, other plants from southeastern Asia were cultivated at that time for use in making rope. These plants—manila, sisal, and jute—produced strong fibers, and less work was needed to extract the fibers. It became cheaper to import rope made of those fibers than to manufacture rope from hemp in the United States.

As a source of fiber for clothing, hemp also lost out to cotton in the 1800s. With the invention of the cotton gin, the process of extracting seeds from cotton bolls was simplified. It made more economic sense to grow cotton than hemp. Part of that "economic sense" also concerned the enslaved Africans, who did most of the labor to prepare cotton and hemp for sale. The cotton gin enabled slaves to produce more cotton for market, so they were moved from hemp fields to cotton fields.

The abolition of slavery after the Civil War freed the enslaved workforce needed to harvest and prepare hemp. The years after the war also brought another change to the use of hemp: the age of steel. Steel cables and wires were many times stronger than any natural plant fiber and became more widely used. By the 1930s, synthetic fibers, such as nylon, were used to make rope. The once amazingly useful plant faded from American agriculture.

FROM HEMP TO MARIJUANA

Although cannabis was not used as an intoxicant in the 1800s in the United States, it was used in some forms as a medicine. In those days, there were no federal laws about ingredients in medicine, and many contained addictive drugs such as morphine and cocaine. Those dangerous drugs became especially common in "health tonics" sold by traveling salesmen. It is believed that by 1900, between 2% and 5% of the U.S. population was addicted to those drugs. During the mid 1800s, marijuana and hashish in various forms (smoked or in liquids) were also common medicines. The Ohio Medical Society reported in 1857 that people using cannabis products claimed that it cured "hysteria . . . whooping cough, asthma . . . chronic bronchitis . . . muscular spasms, epilepsy . . . and appetite [loss]."

In the early 1900s, the federal government passed the Pure Food and Drug Act, which was the first law

Marijuana From Past to Present

to control ingredients in medicines. Although the law didn't mention cannabis, it was the first time that drug use of any kind came under government control. It also introduced the idea of punishing people for drug use.

During the same era, a revolution took place in Mexico. Thousands of Mexicans fled to the United States to avoid the fighting that tore that country apart. Some of the immigrants who came were people who smoked the dried leaves of the cannabis plant, which they called *marijuana*. It was the first time that this everyday term for cannabis and hemp was used in the United States. Although most Americans knew the terms *cannabis* and *hemp*, the term *marijuana* and its use by newcomers led to an anti-immigrant backlash. In 1915, several states in the Southwest passed anti-marijuana laws. In Texas, one lawmaker in favor of the law said, "This stuff makes Mexicans crazy."

Few white Americans at that time had ever heard of marijuana. But by 1919, when a federal law was passed prohibiting alcohol, an editorial in the *New York Times* said this:

> No one here in New York uses this drug marijuana. We have only just heard about it from down in the Southwest . . . [lawmakers] had better prohibit its use before it gets here. Otherwise all the heroin and hard narcotics addicts cut off from their drug . . . and all the alcohol drinkers cut off from their drug by 1919 Prohibition will substitute this new and unknown drug marijuana for the drugs they used to use.

In 1932, the federal prohibition against alcohol use was ended. The laws had not stopped people from drinking. By that time, many Mexican immigrants had moved to large cities in the Midwest and Northeast to work in factories. In cities such as Chicago and New York City, the use of marijuana spread to African Americans, who had also moved to northern cities to work in industry.

The 1930s were a period known as the Great Depression, when more that 25% of the U.S. workforce was jobless. During that time, bad feelings arose among many white workers who believed that Mexicans and African Americans were taking jobs that "belonged" to white people. Like the earlier backlash during the Mexican Revolution, minorities were accused of being criminals and using drugs. At that time, marijuana was linked to drugs such as heroin and cocaine. In 1937, the U.S. Congress passed the Marihuana Tax Act ("marihuana" was the spelling most often used in federal government documents at the time), making the possession of marijuana a federal offense that was punishable by being sent to prison.

Despite harsh penalties, marijuana use spread. Marijuana, also called "reefer" at the time, became popular with jazz musicians and some Hollywood actors. Few white Americans, however, used marijuana—or even used that name for it. In 1945, *Newsweek* magazine wrote that "over 100,000 Americans have used cannabis."

MARIJUANA USE SPREADS TO YOUTH

The years after World War II ended were the beginning of a time known as the Cold War. Many Americans worried that the United States was in danger of attack from communist nations such as China and the Soviet Union (made up of present-day Russia and many smaller countries in Eastern Europe and Asia). Some Americans feared that communists would sneak into the United States to weaken American youth with drugs. Harry Anslinger, commissioner of the Federal Bureau of Narcotics, testified to Congress about the danger of communists

Harry J. Anslinger, commissioner of the Federal Bureau of Narcotics, poses on September 24, 1930. He held this office for 32 years and is considered to be the United States government's first "drug czar"—an official in charge of the country's drug-control policies.

giving drugs—especially marijuana—to American youth. Anslinger, who had once claimed that marijuana made people violent, now said that marijuana actually made

SHOULD MARIJUANA BE LEGALIZED?

In the 1930s, few Americans were familiar with the term *marijuana*. Many learned about the drug from misleading information in newspapers or false testimony from government leaders. As a result, penalties for the use of marijuana were extremely harsh. In those days, there was no debate: Marijuana was a deadly drug, and punishment for its use should be harsh.

Today, attitudes about marijuana have somewhat changed. Some marijuana users believe that the drug should be legalized in the way that alcohol and tobacco are legalized. They argue that legalization would:

- allow society to take money currently spent on the investigation, prosecution, and punishment of drug offenders and use it for more important law enforcement, such as national security
- prevent prison overcrowding
- reduce the amount of drug money received by organized crime
- lower drug-related crime rates
- encourage research into medicinal uses of marijuana
- make tax money from marijuana a source of government income, just like taxes on alcohol and tobacco

Marijuana From Past to Present

Yet, some people oppose legalization. They argue that:

- marijuana is a gateway drug, and that marijuana users are likely to experiment with more dangerous drugs
- there are known health hazards from marijuana consumption
- using marijuana makes workers less productive
- people may use marijuana in risky situations such as driving a car or operating machinery
- airline pilots, train engineers, nuclear power plant operators, and other workers in responsible situations could put the lives of many people at risk if they use marijuana
- the health risks associated with marijuana use are not fully understood

"Smoking marijuana impairs learning and interferes with memory, perception, and judgment," according to the Office of National Drug Control Policy. "Marijuana is also associated with gateway behavior leading to more extensive drug use. This poses serious concerns given the increase in marijuana use by teenagers."

people so peaceful that communists "could and would use marijuana to weaken our . . . will to fight."

These fears led Congress and many states to pass anti-marijuana laws that called for extremely harsh prison sentences. In Virginia, for example, possession of any amount of marijuana resulted in an automatic sentence of 20 years without parole. At the time—the early 1950s—most marijuana users were jazz and blues musicians, or social dropouts known as beatniks. There was little chance that the average white American would go to jail for marijuana possession. But that soon changed.

From the mid 1950s to the late 1960s, an upheaval in U.S. society changed the entire path of marijuana use in the United States. One of the most important changes was rock and roll music. This music helped to bring together young people of all races. At the same time, young people of all races began to speak out about racial injustice, which had long been a problem in the United States. Added to the tension of the time was an increasingly unpopular war in Vietnam and the assassinations of President John F. Kennedy, Dr. Martin Luther King, Jr., and other important figures of this era.

To many people, the world seemed to be falling apart. Suddenly many young people began to doubt the opinions and attitudes of adults. The combination of music, social change, the assassinations of famous and beloved figures, and an unpopular war had a powerful effect. Many people began to rebel against mainstream society. One way that young people rebelled was by smoking marijuana. As a result, millions of young people began to think of marijuana as being harmless rather than dangerous.

Of course, all of these new marijuana users were in danger of facing harsh drug laws that had been passed in the 1950s. This rapid increase in marijuana use

among white Americans led to federal laws that placed marijuana in a new drug category. Marijuana was now dealt with less harshly than illegal and addictive drugs such as heroin, and more harshly than legal and addictive drugs such as tobacco and alcohol. Laws were still tough for people who sold marijuana, but possession, in some areas, did not result in long prison terms.

4

What Marijuana Does to the Body

Throughout thousands of years, people have used marijuana in many different ways. The attitudes of certain cultures toward this drug have also varied widely. For some societies, it has been a plant with many uses. For other societies, it has been a dangerous and illegal drug.

No matter how people have seen marijuana throughout the years, certain things have not changed. The human body today remains the same as it was thousands of years ago. Likewise, marijuana has not changed much. Although marijuana plants today are sometimes bred to contain a higher percentage of THC, the plant's chemical makeup remains the same as it always was. And the body is affected in the same way today when

What Marijuana Does to the Body

marijuana is smoked, eaten, or consumed as a liquid as it was in ancient China and India.

THC, the cannabinoid that causes a "high," is the chemical that affects the body. What follows is a closer look at the way certain parts of the human body react when a person uses marijuana. Since marijuana is most commonly smoked, the lungs are the best place to start.

HOW THE LUNGS WORK

Most people don't think about breathing. It's not necessary because the body does it automatically, breathing in and out—inhaling and exhaling—between 15 and 25 times per minute. This action takes place so that people can inhale oxygen, which the human body's cells need to function. Exhaling gets rid of carbon dioxide, a poisonous gas and a waste product of cells. The lungs do most of this hard work. They are located within the chest cavity and are protected by the rib cage. The lungs are made of soft tissue that stretches as a person inhales and shrinks as a person exhales.

Basically, this is what happens with every breath: Air containing oxygen enters the nose or mouth. It travels to the trachea, or windpipe, until it reaches the bronchi, which look a bit like the branches of a bush. From the bronchi, air passes into each lung. It follows narrower and narrower bronchioles, which are like smaller roads off the main highway of the bronchi. Eventually the air gets to the end of a bronchiole and reaches a tiny air sac called the alveolus. Lungs have millions of **alveoli**, where inhaled and exhaled gases—oxygen and carbon dioxide—trade places. Oxygen enters the bloodstream at those points and continues to the heart, brain, and the rest of the body. Carbon dioxide leaves the bloodstream,

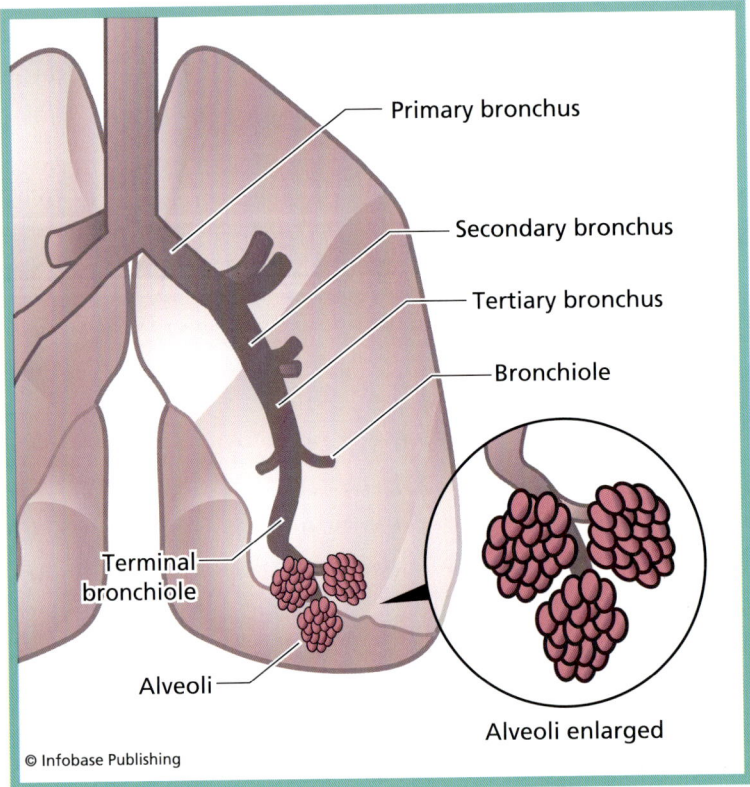

Alveoli are tiny air sacs inside the lungs. When marijuana is inhaled and passes to the lungs, alveoli move the drug into a person's bloodstream.

crosses into the alveoli, and leaves the body when a person exhales.

MARIJUANA AND THE LUNGS

People who smoke any substance take in the drug's chemical smoke in the same way that they take in oxygen: They inhale. Scientists say that smoking is the fastest way for people to feel the effects of THC. When marijuana smoke is inhaled, the THC travels the same pathway as oxygen—trachea to bronchi to bronchiole

What Marijuana Does to the Body

to alveoli. Alveoli are the gateway for THC and other chemicals to enter the bloodstream. The inhaled smoke carries THC and the hundreds of other chemicals in marijuana into the bloodstream in seconds.

Because the lungs are the "border" between marijuana smoke and the chemicals in the smoke, they are defenseless. What makes this worse is that, in general, people who smoke marijuana inhale deeply and hold the smoke in their lungs for as long as possible. Some researchers believe that the habit of holding smoke in the lungs harms the delicate lung tissue. Researchers say that the smoke is especially irritating to the bronchioles, the narrow, branching passageways that lead to the alveoli. In some cases, heavy marijuana smokers may end up with swollen bronchioles, which make breathing difficult. This results in wheezing, and is a symptom of breathing problems such as bronchitis or asthma. Regular pot smokers often experience breathing problems such as frequent coughing and phlegm buildup.

Another dangerous practice is smoking cigarettes in addition to smoking marijuana. Cigarette smokers who also smoke marijuana are introducing literally thousands of chemicals into their bodies each time they use the drug and follow it with a cigarette. Most tobacco smokers smoke about 10 cigarettes per day, whereas people who smoke marijuana regularly say they average three joints per day. This amount of cigarette smoke combined with frequent marijuana use creates an unhealthy environment in one of the most important parts of the body.

One study of more than 400 frequent marijuana smokers who do not smoke tobacco revealed that these people had more health problems and missed more days of work than nonsmokers. Most often, the marijuana smokers who missed work did so because of breathing problems. Even people who do not smoke marijuana regularly may irritate the lining of the mouth and throat from the harsh smoke. Throat irritation often results in a constant cough.

Researchers have long known that smoking cigarettes can cause lung cancer. Many people have wondered whether smoking marijuana can also cause cancer. For more than 25 years, researchers at the University of California at Los Angeles (UCLA) have studied and compared

MARIJUANA LEADS TO LUNG DAMAGE

One joint may be as damaging to a person's lungs as five cigarettes, according to a 2007 study. Experts at the Medical Research Institute of New Zealand tested 339 people, including those who only smoked marijuana, those who only smoked tobacco, and those who smoked both marijuana and tobacco or neither. The results showed that while those who smoked only tobacco suffered more often from the debilitating lung disease emphysema, those who smoked marijuana also damaged their lungs. Specifically, cannabis smokers damaged the small and large airways of their lungs.

The study, which was published in the medical journal *Thorax*, stated that the amount of joints smoked was directly related to the extent of damage to the lungs. The more joints a person smokes, the more damage the person does to their body. According to the research, one joint was equal to smoking two and a half to five cigarettes in one sitting. "The danger [marijuana] poses to respiratory health

What Marijuana Does to the Body

the lung cells of marijuana-only smokers, tobacco-only smokers, smokers of both, and non-smokers. These researchers have found no evidence that marijuana-only smokers are at risk of lung cancer. The research, however, has shown some changes in bronchial cells that have been called "pre-cancerous," which means that it is possible that heavy marijuana smokers (smoking more than five **joints** daily) have an increased risk of cancer.

Joints are cigarettes filled with the leaves and flower buds of the marijuana plant. Usually special rolling paper, which comes in different sizes and flavors, is used to wrap the drug.

is consistently being overlooked," said Helena Shovelton, chief executive of the British Lung Foundation.

Hemp enthusiast Andrew Seidenfeld promotes the usage of hemp. Here, he holds hemp bread at a stand promoting hemp products in December 2001 in New York City.

EATING MARIJUANA

Marijuana can also be eaten or consumed in a drink, such as tea. Some people take marijuana this way because they fear the dangers of smoking. But eating marijuana poses its own dangers. When marijuana is taken into the body this way, THC enters the bloodstream through the stomach. As it does with any food, the stomach produces digestive acids that break down the contents of the stomach into chemicals that can be absorbed into the bloodstream.

Because marijuana is usually mixed with food in order to be eaten, the food must be digested before the THC can be absorbed in the bloodstream. Depending on the amount of food in a person's stomach, digestion can take as long as several hours before the THC is released

What Marijuana Does to the Body

into the bloodstream. And that is the danger that people who eat marijuana encounter. They may think that the marijuana has not worked in their system and will continue to eat more of the drug-laced food. This can put a large amount of THC into their system once the digestive process is complete. This can cause extreme nausea. Some people are unable to talk; others may suffer balance problems from the sudden rush of large amounts of THC. Another danger of eating marijuana is that the effects last many hours longer than when it is smoked. As a result, the user will not be able to feel or act normally for quite a long time.

CIRCULATORY SYSTEM

After smoking or eating marijuana, its chemicals travel deeper into the body through the circulatory system. This includes the arteries, veins, and capillaries, which run through the body like a system of rivers and streams. The heart pumps blood through the body to all its organs. The blood provides nutrients to cells in the body and also rids those cells of waste.

The bloodstream of an adult human contains about five quarts of blood. The blood itself is made up of cells and **plasma**. Plasma is the liquid part of the blood and is the color of hay when it is separated from blood cells, which it carries. There are two kinds of blood cells: red and white. Red blood cells, which give blood its color, carry oxygen from the lungs to the cells and remove carbon dioxide from the cells. White blood cells fight infections as part of the immune system. Platelets, another part of the blood, are cells that the body uses to clot and stop bleeding. Plasma also carries life-giving vitamins and minerals—as well as chemicals such as THC.

When THC and the many other chemicals in marijuana enter the bloodstream, they pass through the liver.

This large organ filters out waste and stores it in its fatty tissue. This is one way that drug tests can reveal whether a person has used marijuana. Because THC collects in the liver, a blood test can detect the drug in a person's body as long as a month after it has been used.

The most important piece of the circulatory system is the heart. The heart, a hollow muscle, sits between the lungs and beats about three or four times faster per minute (72 times) than a person breathes (about 20 times.) Each time a person breathes, oxygen goes from the lungs, through the chambers of the heart, and out to the organs through the heart's aorta, the major artery exiting the heart. Each time a person exhales, blood from the pulmonary veins flows into the heart, and then to the lungs. For this reason, the system that includes the lungs and heart is known as the pulmonary system.

THC has an effect on the heart and circulation no matter how it enters the body. When it enters through the lungs, it causes the heart to race 20 to 50 beats per minute faster. This causes the blood vessels in the eyes to expand, causing the whites of the eyes to become red, a sign of marijuana use. The effect of THC on the heart can be even greater if other drugs, such as nicotine from tobacco, are used at the same time. The THC in marijuana can also cause chest pain in some people whose circulatory systems are weak.

THE BRAIN

If THC affected only the lungs and heart, chances are its use would not have become as widespread as it has. It is the effect of THC on the brain that makes it desirable to some people.

To understand how marijuana affects the brain, it is important to know about the structure of the brain.

The brain is made up of billions of cells called **neurons**. The actions of these cells are what allow information to be processed and thoughts, feelings, and actions to take place. In some cases, it is information that is conscious, such as remembering arithmetic rules. In other cases, it is unconscious, such as the message from the brain that tells the body to jump in a game of basketball.

Neurons "talk" to each other through chemical messengers called **neurotransmitters**. These chemicals fill the spaces, called synapses, between neurons. Some neurons have endings, called receptors, that are sensitive to certain neurotransmitters. One kind of receptor that is found in several locations in the brain is the **cannabinoid receptor**. Cannabinoid receptors are set in motion by a neurotransmitter called anandamide, which is a cannabinoid that occurs naturally in the body.

Cannabinoid receptors are found in three main areas of the brain: the **hippocampus, cerebellum**, and **basal ganglia**. The hippocampus is the place in which short-term memory takes place. The cerebellum helps controls coordination. And the basal ganglia control unconscious muscle movements.

Given this basic information, it should come as no surprise what happens when a person uses marijuana. Researchers in the 1960s discovered that THC, which is also a cannabinoid, imitates neurotransmitters or in some cases stops them from completing their normal activity. Instead of the natural activity between anandamide and cannabinoid receptors, THC takes over and causes the mind and body to change.

For example, when THC interacts with the cannabinoid receptors of the hippocampus, the marijuana user forgets events that have just happened. It becomes difficult to concentrate on something as simple as reading a page in a book. Moods change from happiness to fear

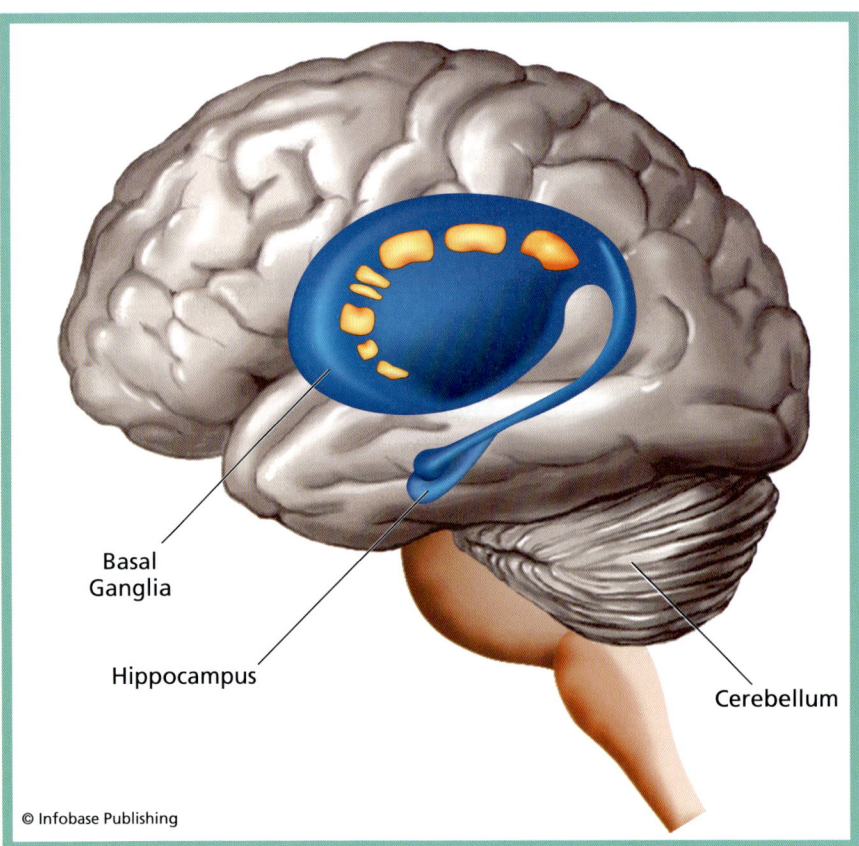

Marijuana use affects the brain and, therefore, the body. When people smoke marijuana, cannabinoid receptors bind to neurotransmitters and initiate a cellular response—in other words, they create biological changes. The receptors are mainly found in the hippocampus, cerebellum, and basal ganglia.

and back again rapidly. When THC interacts with the neurons of the cerebellum, it affects the coordination necessary for athletic activity. There is also a changed perception of time. People who smoke marijuana often describe feeling hazy and light-headed. The pupils of their eyes, partially controlled by the basal ganglia, may open wide. This causes colors to appear brighter. Other senses such as taste, touch, and hearing are also changed.

MEDICAL USE OF MARIJUANA

Research has shown that smoking marijuana can cause many negative health effects, from memory loss to respiratory problems. Yet, there are many Americans who believe that marijuana has important uses as a medicine. Cannabis was commonly used as a medicine in the United States during the 1800s. In fact, before the invention of aspirin, cannabis was most often used as a cure for headaches.

In the 1960s and 1970s, marijuana use became widespread, and people with certain health conditions discovered that marijuana—which was illegal by then—soothed them. Some people with the eye condition known as

A proponent of medical marijuana holds a sign outside of the U.S. Supreme Court in Washington, DC. In 2005, the court ruled that doctors could be blocked from prescribing marijuana for patients suffering from pain caused by cancer or other serious illnesses.

(continues on page 68)

(continued from page 67)

glaucoma found that smoking marijuana lessened painful pressure in the eyeball. U.S. troops who suffered spinal injuries during the Vietnam War found that smoking marijuana lessened painful muscles spasms. Cancer patients found that marijuana lessened the nausea they suffered from drugs used in anti-cancer treatment.

Drug researchers during that time were able to produce a copy of THC in pill form, called Marinol. This drug copied the effects of THC, but did not make users high. But Marinol cost thousands of dollars per month, much more than marijuana bought illegally.

Research into the use of medical marijuana by the Institute of Medicine (IOM) of the U.S. National Academy of Sciences has found that marijuana can indeed help prevent nausea and vomiting. The research has not discovered the exact reason why this works. Other research has found that marijuana is a mild yet effective pain reliever against headache and muscle injury. The reason for this also remains unknown, but "the accumulated data indicate a potential therapeutic value for cannabinoid drugs for pain relief, control of nausea and vomiting, and appetite stimulation," according to an IOM report in 1999.

A majority of Americans of all ages favor making medical marijuana legally available to doctors to prescribe. As of 2006, 11 states had passed laws allowing doctors to do so. In 2005, however, the U.S. Supreme Court ruled that state marijuana laws did not protect users from federal laws against the drug.

5

What Marijuana Does to the Mind

Allan (not his real name) got stoned for the first time when he was 17. He didn't like the harsh smoke, and coughed a few times as he tried to hold it in. He almost turned down the joint the third time it came around to him as it was passed from an older friend. But as he inhaled that third time, the lit end of the joint glowed brightly. He could hear the sound of smoke crackling through the rolled leaves. The songs playing on the CD suddenly sounded better than he remembered. This time, the smoke did not taste so harsh. And when he tried to pass the joint to his friend next to him, it fell out of his hands. Allan thought that was one of the funniest things he had ever seen. He laughed so hard he could hardly catch his breath.

A year later, Allan had finished high school. At one time he had planned to go to the college in his town, but he never got around to applying. He lived at home with his parents and worked unloading trucks at a discount store. He tried to learn the guitar, but he never got past learning the same three chords over and over. Then he stopped practicing.

One thing Allan did do regularly was smoke pot. He smoked every day. Sometimes he smoked all day. Getting stoned was his first thought in the morning. Sometimes he smoked on the way to work. He often smoked at lunch, and if he didn't smoke then, he lit a joint as he drove home. When he wasn't high, he thought about getting high. Allan was very rarely out of his supply of pot, and when he was, he became extremely anxious. It was his drug of choice, and he didn't believe it was harmful.

THE PULL OF POT

Many books and articles talk about the dangers of marijuana smoking. They talk about the effect on the lungs, the heart, and other organs. They warn people about the dangers that can come from using marijuana. These effects and warnings are all true. Yet, people still use the drug because they want to experience its immediate physical effects.

Scientists use the term *psychoactive* to describe chemicals that cause changes in the brain. Marijuana is made up of more than 400 chemicals, but only THC is considered "psychoactive." It is the interaction between THC and cannabinoid receptors in the brain that makes marijuana a drug that attracts so many users. Once THC enters the bloodstream, its effects take only a few seconds. That's why Allan saw bright colors and heard faint buzzing sounds when the joint was passed around for the third time. By that time, he had started to feel the high. This is often described as a floating feeling, a feeling of drifting away from "real" life. People who use marijuana may describe the feeling as relaxed.

A marijuana smoker who continues to smoke after this first phase may reach the point where the level of

THE MUNCHIES

One unusual side effect of marijuana use is increased hunger. This phenomenon has long been known and is popularly called the "munchies." Research by the National Institutes of Health has shown that smoking marijuana increases food enjoyment and may increase the number of times a person eats each day.

For many years, the explanation for the munchies was unknown. Then, in the late 1990s, research by Italian scientists helped to explain how using marijuana increases the appetite. The research showed that THC interacts with cannabinoid receptors in the brain's hypothalamus. These receptors are normally responsible for controlling the appetite. The interaction with THC sets them off and makes people hungry even if they have already eaten.

This can of course lead to an overly full and upset stomach, as well as unwanted weight gain. Users of medical marijuana, however, might consider increased appetite a benefit. Cancer patients and people with HIV/AIDS often lose their appetites during drug treatments for those diseases. Weight loss is a serious problem for these people. The increased appetite that comes with using marijuana can help these people maintain a healthy weight.

THC in his brain has made him feel the high. In this state, actions and words may seem extremely funny. The mind may jump from thought to thought for no reason. A person might laugh uncontrollably one moment, and then cry out in fear the next. Music may seem richer in sound and people may hear parts of familiar songs that they had never noticed before. "Being high was like moving from black-and-white movies to full color," said one person who used marijuana a few times before quitting. "It made ordinary life special and made me see things that I normally took for granted in a new way."

Users who continue to smoke and consume more than the equivalent of one or two joints at one time reach a state most commonly known as "stoned." In this state, the earlier symptoms of the high are usually more intense. People become emotional—friendly and talkative in some cases or sad and fearful in others. Their eyes are often squinted shut or red and dry. Some people may become very lazy and remain seated in one place for hours until the effect wears off. They may feel extremely hungry and consume large quantities of food. All of this occurs because of the effect of THC on cannabinoid receptors.

THE DAMAGE MARIJUANA DOES

Certainly, intoxicants of any kind, illegal or legal, can be bad for the body. Tobacco has been proven to cause lung cancer. Alcohol has been linked to liver disease, heart problems, throat cancer, and other serious health problems. And tobacco, alcohol, and drugs such as heroin and cocaine have also been proven to be physically addictive. Studies have shown that the brain develops a tolerance to those drugs and, over time, more of the drug is needed to satisfy cravings. THC, on the other hand, activates cannabinoid receptors at the same levels whether a person smokes marijuana once or has smoked for years. This means that a person does not develop a higher tolerance to marijuana over time.

Given all of this information, the question people might ask is, what is it about marijuana that makes it harmful? The answer is that the very feelings that using marijuana creates—the high—can also bring on problems. The "stoned" feeling created by the THC usually fades after about two hours. But chemicals formed by the interaction of THC and the cannabinoid receptors stay in the body for days and sometimes weeks.

Thus, people who smoke marijuana regularly are continually keeping THC and its by-products in their bodies. They may not feel stoned, but even short-term regular use can lead to problems such as a constant feeling of sleepiness. They may become couch potatoes who have very little energy. This constant feeling of "dragging" can lead to depression, say health professionals—a lack of motivation, or "amotivational syndrome." Marijuana users can therefore develop a poor self-image. They stop caring about their lives and do not care about what they do.

Some users may experience more serious mental problems. Research shows that people who used marijuana weekly during their teenage years have an increased risk of depression later in life. This is especially true of female marijuana users who started as teens. Research shows that girls with no history of depression or anxiety who use marijuana are five times more likely to be depressed at age 21 than non-users.

Marijuana use can also give rise to thoughts of suicide. A study based on the National Household Survey on Drug Abuse found that people between the ages of 12 and 17 who smoke marijuana once per week are three times more likely than non-users of the same age

MARIJUANA'S MENTAL COSTS

Scientists have proven that there is a connection between marijuana use and an increased chance of having psychotic (mental) disorders, such as schizophrenia. In a 2007 study sponsored by the British Health Department and published in the medical journal *The Lancet*, researchers noted that people who use marijuana have an approximately 40% higher chance of developing a psychotic disorder. Plus, regular users—those who smoke marijuana daily or weekly—have a 50% to 200% increased risk for having a mental illness.

"The available evidence now suggests that cannabis is not as harmless as many people think," said Dr. Stanley Zammit, one of the study's authors and a lecturer in the department of psychological medicine at Cardiff University in Wales, United Kingdom.

To conduct the 2007 study, researchers examined 35 studies, which focused on tens of thousands of people for a period of time ranging from one year to 27 years, in order to study the effects of marijuana on mental health. Yet, scientists have not ruled out that pre-existing mental conditions could have led to psychosis. "Marijuana use could unmask the underlying schizophrenia," explains Dr. Deepak Cyril D'Souza, an associate professor of psychiatry at Yale University, who was not involved in the study. Whether or not a person already has a pre-existing mental condition, this study proves that marijuana increases a person's risk for psychosis or at least exposes and perhaps worsens underlying psychotic disorders.

to have suicidal thoughts. The same study reported that marijuana use resulted in increased anxiety and panic attacks. Even more serious, studies have connected marijuana use with symptoms of schizophrenia, a disease in which people hear voices and may commit irrational acts. Heavy users of marijuana at age 18 increased their risk of schizophrenia later in life by six times. Early heavy use of marijuana—age 15 instead of age 18—increased the risk even more.

Marijuana users may also have problems with short-term memory. They forget names of people they have just met. They leave behind a bag or a wallet or keys and don't recall where they have been. They are often late for classes or work because their weak short-term memory affects their sense of time. In fact, many of the mental skills that are most necessary for young people to do well in school are the skills most affected by marijuana use. Users may not be able to concentrate when others—such as teachers—are speaking. They may have difficulty remembering important facts or solving complicated problems.

As previously mentioned, researchers have found that adolescent brains have a "growth spurt" as they enter puberty. That's why many health professionals agree that the younger a person is when he or she first smokes marijuana, the greater the risk that he or she will exhibit the symptoms above at one of the most crucial times for human development.

Marijuana use affects day-to-day life outside of the classroom as well. All of the difficulties mentioned above are skills needed on a job, too. In addition, marijuana use may reduce a person's ability to perform activities that require concentration and coordination, such as running dangerous machinery. In 1987, for example, a

MARIJUANA

Workers sifted through wreckage of an Amtrak train that was derailed on January 4, 1987 near Baltimore, Maryland. The train's engineer had been smoking marijuana on the job.

passenger train derailed in Maryland, killing 14 people. Tests showed that both the engineer and a crewmember responsible for watching track change signals had been using marijuana.

THE YOUNG BRAIN

For many years, scientists believed that most of the growth in the human brain occurred in the first three years of life. A baby's brain during that time makes more brain cells and connections than he or she can use. Those cells and connections are cut back around the age of three, which strengthens the cells and connections that are left. This "cutting back" was believed to end in the brain by age six.

In recent years, however, the development of new medical technology has allowed scientists to more closely study the ways that the brain grows and works. Using this new technology, scientists see what parts of the brain use energy during certain tasks.

Dr. Jay Giedd, a researcher at the National Institute of Mental Health in Bethesda, Maryland, has discovered a second period of cell and connection growth beginning at age 11 in girls and 12 in boys. This is followed by a cutting away period, and then a growth in the front part of the brain beginning at about age 13. The hippocampus is located in this area, an area that controls organizing, memory, and moods. As this part of the brain grows during the teenage years, young people can develop their ability to control their moods and make judgments.

According to Giedd, the act of cutting away is a healthy process that leaves the remaining cells and connections strengthened. He believes that it is a particularly important stage of brain development. What teens do to affect their brains makes a huge difference in their lives. Positive activities, such as learning to play an instrument or reading about new subjects and ideas, help brain development. Negative activities, such as smoking, drinking, or using other drugs, keep the brain from being all it can be. "If a teen is doing music or sports or academics, those are the cells and connections that will be hard-wired," Giedd says. "If they're lying on the couch or playing video games or MTV, those are the cells and connections that are going [to] survive."

In addition to changes in the front part of the brain, Giedd's research also found second waves of growth in the system of nerve fibers that connect the sides of the brain. This is the area of the brain that affects language skills and creative thinking—the imagination "lives" there. The cerebellum also grows during adolescence. This is the area that helps in physical coordination, and it is also important in the development of skills such as music, math, and decision-making.

All three of the areas described here contain cannabinoid receptors. For this reason, it is especially unhealthy for young people to smoke marijuana, say drug researchers.

Because the chemical effects of marijuana remain in the brain, many of the risks described above remain after people stop smoking. In one study of college students, scientists took 65 "heavy users," who had smoked marijuana about 29 of the previous 30 days, and compared them against 64 "light users." The people described as light users had smoked one day out of the past 30 days. After a closely watched, 24-hour period in which the students remained free of marijuana (as well as other illegal drugs and alcohol), students were given tests that measured attention, memory, and learning. Heavy marijuana users made more mistakes and had more difficulty understanding and using information.

Scientists say that research on marijuana use among high school students shows that those who used marijuana have lower achievement than the non-users. Users are also more likely to show destructively rebellious behavior, have poor relationships with parents, and associate with delinquent or drug-using peers.

PSYCHOLOGICAL ADDICTION

In 1970, a panel funded by the U.S. government studied the question of marijuana addiction. According to this group, known as the Shafer Commission, "Marijuana does not lead to physical dependency, although some evidence indicates that long-term users may develop a psychological dependence on the drug."

What Marijuana Does to the Mind

Research since then has backed up the Shafer Commission statement that marijuana is not physically addictive. That does not mean that people cannot become addicted to its use—that is, to feel a need to be stoned. Allan, at the beginning of this chapter, was a person whom drug counselors would label as "psychologically

GATEWAY DRUGS

Research results conflict over whether using marijuana leads people to use harder drugs.

Many people believe its relatively easy availability and lure make it accessible, thereby encouraging users to try other drugs. Some research by the National Institute on Drug Abuse (NIDA), however, says that this is not the case. The institute's research indicates that it is early use of tobacco that leads to use of marijuana. On the other hand, research by the American Medical Association (AMA) indicates that smoking marijuana, especially for people younger than age 17, may lead to harder drug use. According to the AMA, young people who smoke marijuana are two to five times more likely to move on to harder drugs. The AMA study followed 311 sets of identical twins; in each pair, one twin smoked marijuana but the other did not. Twins were chosen to help rule out a genetic or social explanation for the gateway effect. Almost half of the twins who started smoking marijuana before age 17 went on to use harder drugs later in life. Thus, although not everyone agrees with the idea that marijuana is a gateway drug, there is just not enough evidence to prove for sure that it is not.

addicted" to marijuana. In many ways, psychological addiction can be as serious as physical addiction. In fact, addiction experts today no longer separate psychological and physical dependence. What matters, they say, is whether a person's need for a drug causes uncontrollable drug-seeking and use. Even when a person is addicted to taking a legal drug, health and social problems may result. Researchers call this "drug hunger." It is in some ways more difficult to manage than physical cravings, which can sometimes be managed with medical treatment.

Getting Help

In seventh grade, Savannah (not her real name) looked older than she was. With older kids, she often pretended to know more than she really did about drugs and other dangerous behaviors. Her parents were divorced, and her mom sometimes smoked pot with adult friends. Savannah thought smoking pot was what adults did. When some high school students she hung out with started talking about pot, she nodded her head when they said it was no big deal. When they passed around a pipe, Savannah didn't want to seem like a child, so she got stoned. That was the beginning of a long period of bad choices.

"I was running with older kids, guys," she said. "I wasn't doing much in school but no one else was either. I got stoned because I wanted to fit in. Pretty soon, getting stoned was my answer to every problem in my life."

WHAT IS ADDICTION?

Most people would agree that Savannah made a bad decision to smoke marijuana. And it led to other bad decisions. She dropped out of high school at age 16 and began a period of several years in which she made one mistake after another. Savannah felt a daily need to smoke marijuana, no matter what. But although most readers might agree that Allan and Savannah were in trouble, those same readers might be uncertain about whether to call them addicts.

Part of that uncertainty arises from the fact that "addiction" is sometimes used today in ways that make it seem like a joke. A person might say, "I'm addicted to that TV show" or, "I'm addicted to shopping" or, "I'm addicted to Coffee Almond Fudge ice cream." In other words, people use the word *addiction* to exaggerate, for laughs. But drug addiction is not funny. It destroys lives. Physical addiction leads to crime and death. And addiction to tobacco and alcohol—legal for adults—is responsible for more deaths than crack, heroin, and meth combined.

So where does that leave marijuana? There is no proof that smoking marijuana causes a physical need for more and more of the drug so that a smoker will feel "normal," as is the case with physically addictive drugs such as crack. Yet, many health professionals agree that marijuana users may find themselves psychologically addicted to the drug. Although smokers do not need ever larger quantities of marijuana to become high, they don't feel right unless they are stoned most of the time.

In some ways, it does not matter whether an addiction is physical or psychological; the outcome is often similar. An addict continues to use a drug even when using it has negative consequences. Crack users and alcoholics risk death in many different and sometimes violent ways when they smoke or drink. Cigarette smokers risk serious health problems that could lead to cancer or other killer diseases. Marijuana users risk physical, social, and legal problems that often ruin their lives. Yet they continue to use. Allan and Savannah are examples of such people.

Even famous people are not immune to the consequences of marijuana use. Consider the case of pro-football player Ricky Williams. His actions have harmed him in ways that few people can imagine. Williams was a star football player from childhood through college. Big, strong, and fast, he was a running back who won the award for being the best player in college football in 1999. He was drafted into pro football and signed a contract worth millions of dollars.

Williams, however, also smoked marijuana all through high school and college. There were no drug tests at those levels of the sport, so his actions off the field didn't hurt him on the field—until he became a professional player. The National Football League (NFL) tests players for drugs. In 2002, Williams was the leading rusher in the NFL. But by then he had failed two drug tests for marijuana. He failed his third test in 2004, just after he signed a contract worth $8 million. Instead of facing punishment from the NFL, Williams retired from pro football. "The thing that I had the most trouble with was that after you fail your third test, then it becomes public knowledge that you failed the test," he said. "And that's the one thing that I couldn't deal with at the time. People knowing that I smoke marijuana. That was my biggest fear in my whole entire life. I was scared to death of that."

(continues on page 86)

Miami Dolphins running back Ricky Williams signs autographs for fans after playing a scrimmage with the Tennessee Titans on August 2, 2003 in Nashville, Tennessee. After repeatedly failing drug tests for marijuana use, Williams was suspended from the game in 2006. In October 2007, he applied for reinstatement with the NFL and was reinstated a month later based on clean tests.

Getting Help 85

TESTING FOR MARIJUANA USE

Each year about 20 million workers in the United States are tested for drugs. As Ricky Williams has learned the hard way, there are very accurate tests used today to determine whether a person has used marijuana. The main reason for that is the THC in marijuana. As THC travels through the bloodstream, it is absorbed in the fatty tissue of organs such as the liver and kidneys. It may remain there for as long as three months. From the fatty tissues of body organs, the body changes THC into about five different chemicals before it passes into the body's urine. Drug

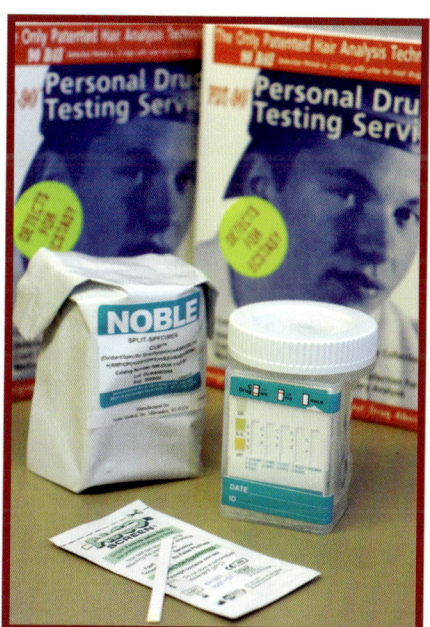

Home drug-testing kits from the company Test My Teen are displayed. The products test for traces of drugs or alcohol in a body. Both schools and parents have purchased the tests for use.

(continues on page 86)

(continued from page 85)

tests are designed to discover the presence of those chemicals, called metabolites. The accuracy of drug tests is different from person to person, depending on how long they have been smoking, how much they have smoked, and how high the marijuana's THC content was.

There are a few tests that are used to detect marijuana use. The test that is used most often to determine marijuana use is called the immuno-assay test. In this process, urine is mixed with a solution containing a dye that glows when it comes into contact with a THC metabolite. Another test that is used is a test of human hair. THC metabolites pass through the blood vessels in the head and collect permanently in hair. Since the average human hair grows about one-half of an inch (1.25 cm) per month, the THC metabolites remain unless a person shaves his or her head. The hair test is rarely used, though, because it costs about $200. An immuno-assay test is cheaper—about $65.

(continued from page 83)

Williams returned to football one year later. But he failed a fourth drug test for marijuana. The NFL suspended Williams for the 2006 season. He had planned to return to the NFL in the 2007 season, but in May 2007, he failed another drug test for marijuana use. After finally passing a drug test and being reinstated to the NFL, 30-year-old Williams was injured in his first game back with the Dolphins in November 2007. His torn chest muscle injury left him out for the rest of the season. At 30 years old, Williams sat the majority of the 2007 season out, knowing he was a bit old for an NFL player. Williams admits that he wasted a lot of time because of drug use and he may have few healthy years left. There is little doubt that his career has been damaged by his inability to stop smoking marijuana. Was he addicted to the drug? Some people would say yes because his use got in the way of his life.

HOW CAN ADDICTS CHANGE?

For years, many people thought of addicts as people who didn't have the "courage" to change their behavior. They were seen as weak or in some cases "bad" because of their continued use of a drug or multiple drugs. In recent years, however, many health professionals have considered addiction—both physical and psychological—to be a disease. They say that addiction is often passed down through generations. There are often common personality traits among addicts, no matter what drug or drugs he or she uses. Addicts are often isolated and uncomfortable in social situations if they are not high. Many have low self-confidence. They only feel "normal" under the influence of their drug of choice. Most try to hide their problem because they are ashamed of feeling "weak."

People who are addicted to marijuana are totally focused on getting high, even when they know that using it could lead to personal disaster, as it did with Ricky Williams. Marijuana addicts often promise loved ones that they will stop using the drug, but soon fall back into their habit after a short period of time. And they break the same promise again and again. It is a condition psychologists call "chronic relapsing," and it comes from an addict's inability to face life without the "crutch" of marijuana.

Many marijuana addicts deny that they have a problem at all, even when their lives are falling apart because of their inability to stop smoking. One way for a person to determine if he or she is a marijuana addict is to answer a series of questions about drug use. These questions were developed by a group called **Marijuana Anonymous (MA)**. This group follows ideas developed in the 1930s by an organization called Alcoholics Anonymous (AA). People who belong to MA meet in small groups to share their experiences with one another. Often, meeting in groups helps addicts understand that they do not have to face their problems alone. They stay drug- or alcohol-free by turning to others and joining forces to recover from their addictions.

Members of MA admit they have an addiction to marijuana and try to stay away from the drug by helping others to stay away from it as well. To anyone who is uncertain whether his or her use of marijuana is an addiction, MA suggests answering the following 12 questions:

1. Has smoking pot stopped being fun?
2. Do you ever get high alone?
3. Is it hard for you to imagine a life without marijuana?
4. Do you find that your friends are determined by your marijuana use?
5. Do you smoke marijuana to avoid dealing with your problems?
6. Do you smoke pot to cope with your feelings?
7. Does your marijuana use let you live in a privately defined world?
8. Have you ever failed to keep promises you made about cutting down or controlling your marijuana smoking?

9. Has your use of marijuana caused problems with memory, concentration, or motivation?
10. When your stash is nearly empty, do you feel anxious or worried about how to get more?
11. Do you plan your life around your marijuana use?
12. Have friends or relatives ever complained that your pot smoking is damaging your relationship with them?

MA members say that anyone who answers yes to just *one* of those questions most likely has a psychological addiction to marijuana.

The first step to getting help for marijuana addiction is admitting that drug use is a problem. The next step is giving up the drug. Often that step is very difficult. Withdrawal from marijuana use does not produce physical illness, as occurs with heroin and some other drugs. Still, marijuana addicts do suffer withdrawal symptoms. People trying to quit report feeling irritable and anxious and that they have trouble sleeping. Some addicts who give up smoking claim that they become more aggressive with others after a week away from pot.

These symptoms do not occur only with long-time users. In 2005, psychologists studied 72 teenage marijuana users who were in treatment centers for their addiction. The subjects, mostly white males, were asked to fill out a questionnaire about their experience of withdrawing from daily marijuana use. Almost two-thirds of the teenagers reported signs of withdrawal, such as irritability, anxiety, and aggressiveness. More than one-third described their feelings as intense. These were not addicts who had smoked for year after year into their twenties and thirties. Most had smoked for less than four years.

For many marijuana addicts, no matter how long they have smoke, the experience of withdrawal symptoms combined with the knowledge that they must give up the drug for the rest of their lives is difficult. For that reason, MA advises addicts to think only in terms of not smoking for one day at a time. They recommend that addicts attend 90 MA meetings in the first 90 days of their recovery to talk out their feelings with other recovering addicts. One motto of MA is "*I* can't but *we* can." By attending meetings, marijuana addicts find other people who will understand what they are going through as they try to put together a new life.

Savannah entered the MA recovery program at age 19 after six years of smoking pot nearly every day. Within a year, she had earned her GED (the equivalent to a high school diploma) and found her first full-time job. "At first, I was scared to admit that I was an addict, but pretty soon I looked forward to my MA meetings, to sharing as well as listening," Savannah said. "It is hard to put into words how my life has changed. I am truly happy for the first time. I have never been more proud of anything I have ever done."

WHEN FRIENDS USE MARIJUANA

Marijuana is a large part of life for some people. Even people who try to avoid marijuana are likely to know someone who smokes it. And some people may face a difficult choice when they discover that a friend is a pot smoker. Friendships are important, and close friendships are especially important in life. It's not easy to give up on a friendship when a friend makes a poor choice and uses marijuana. Young people who have no problem keeping away from drugs may find it difficult to convince a friend to do the same.

Psychologists say there are certain ways that a person can persuade a friend to stop smoking. Anyone who answers yes to MA's 12 questions should seek professional help. And if a person has a friend who answers yes to those questions, that person should advise his or her friend to seek help. That's what a good friend does.

Yet, many young people don't believe marijuana is harmful because they have seen other people smoke pot. There are many ways to convince a friend that smoking pot is not cool. One way is to inform the smoker that that he may be smoking more than just marijuana. It is not unusual for some dealers to put strong and even deadly drugs into marijuana. Another approach is to point out that smoking marijuana makes people do dumb things, such as making dangerous choices about sex or riding in cars with people who aren't sober. In fact, telling pot smokers that using marijuana makes them just plain dumb can work, too. And it's true: Pot smokers have been shown to have short-term memory problems and difficulty studying.

Appearance is another way to talk friends out of smoking marijuana. Point out how awful he or she looks with squinty, bloodshot eyes. Remind him or her about the munchies and the possibility for unwanted weight gain. The main idea is to make the smoker understand that getting stoned is not as cool as some people say it is.

Using warnings such as these might help stop a friend from trying marijuana more than once. For most people, quitting is not difficult. But one of the best ways to make sure a person stays pot-free is to suggest other activities to fill free time.

There are plenty of ways to relax without drugs. For example, physical activity often helps to release chemicals in the brain that create a relaxed feeling. Running, skateboarding, bicycling, or playing basketball can all create a feeling of wellbeing without the risks that come with drug use. And those are activities that friends can do together. Playing music is another activity that can take up empty time. This means more than downloading songs. It means being active in things such as singing, putting together a hip-hop track, practicing dance, or starting a band. Making music with other people is a great way to build strong friendships.

Sports and music are just two of many activities that can make friends tighter and keep them from turning to marijuana. There are many other ways to use free time in a useful way. A school or neighborhood project, such as collecting used books for a library sale or gathering bottles for recycling, takes time and benefits the community. Even a part-time job such as yard work, house cleaning, or other odd jobs can earn money and keep friends busy.

In the end, it's possible that none of these suggestions will work. If a friend not only continues smoking, but also tries to convince his or her friends to use marijuana, too, that person may not be the best kind of friend to have. Giving up on a friend is a difficult choice. But any person who decides to use a drug and encourages others to use it, too, is making a wrong turn in life. No friendship is worth taking the risks.

HOW TO AVOID POT

Turning down an offer to smoke marijuana with a person or group of people can sometimes be difficult. Too many young people agree to go along with the pot-smoking crowd because they don't know how to say no and still seem cool. One of the best ways to deal with

Getting Help

HOW TO SAY NO

Some examples of ways to turn down marijuana:

- Explain a personal problem you have with marijuana: It's illegal, there could be other drugs hidden within it, and it hurts brain cells.
- Point out the consequences: getting arrested, family rejection, making a fool of oneself.
- Speak up about personal beliefs. For example:
  "I don't feel the need to do drugs to make you think I'm cool."
  "I have better things to do than smoke."
  "I play sports and this will hurt my lungs. Besides, it can be detected with tests. Look what happened to Ricky Williams."
  "I don't want to hurt people I care about. If my family found out they would be really disappointed."

the pressure to smoke marijuana is to prepare ways to turn it down.

The best idea, of course, is to avoid people, places, and events where the pressure to smoke marijuana might arise. But that is not always possible. Psychologists say that young people who are determined to stay away from marijuana should think ahead about being in an awkward situation with friends or older people who urge them to "just try it."

A FINAL WORD

Marijuana has been used for thousands of years by people in different parts of the world. Yet, even from earliest times, ancient people recognized that cannabis was a substance that could be harmful to some people. Today, scientists continue to find evidence that marijuana use can be risky. Knowledge is the most important tool people can have when deciding whether or not to use a drug. It can also help people help friends who struggle with that same decision.

CHRONOLOGY

10,000 B.C.	Earliest evidence of cannabis being used for fiber is found in Taiwan.
4000 B.C.	Textiles made of hemp are used in China.
2727 B.C.	Use of cannabis as medicine in China is first recorded.
1200–800 B.C.	Bhang (dried cannabis leaves, seeds, and stems) is mentioned in Hindu texts as one of the five sacred plants of India. It is used medicinally and in religious ceremonies.
500 B.C.	Hemp is introduced into northern Europe by the Scythians. An urn containing leaves and seeds of the cannabis plant is unearthed in Germany and dated to about this time.
500–100 B.C.	Hemp spreads throughout northern Europe.
A.D. 70	Dioscorides mentions the use of cannabis as a Roman medicine.
900–1000	Hashish use spreads through Arabian Peninsula.
1200s	Cannabis is introduced in Egypt.
1295	Marco Polo's journeys bring the first reports of cannabis as an intoxicant in Asia to the attention of Europe.
1606–1632	The British cultivate cannabis in their American colonies.
1798	Soldiers returning to France from wars in Egypt bring cannabis and hashish with them.
1840–1900	In the United States, medicines containing cannabis are widely used.
1906	The Pure Food and Drug Act is passed in the United States, regulating the labeling of products containing alcohol, opiates, and cocaine, among other substances.

Chronology

1915–1927 Marijuana begins to be prohibited by states, including California (1915), Texas (1919), Louisiana (1924), and New York (1927).

1937 Cannabis is made illegal nationwide in the United States with the passage of the Marihuana Tax Act.

1972 The Shafer Commission, a federally sponsored group, urges legalization of cannabis in a manner similar to tobacco and alcohol. The recommendation is ignored.

1975 The U.S. Food and Drug Administration establishes a program for medical marijuana.

1988 A Drug Enforcement Administration judge finds that marijuana has medical uses and should be reclassified as a prescriptive drug. His recommendation is ignored. In June 2003, Canada is the first country in the world to offer medical marijuana to its patients.

February 2006 Studies show that marijuana is the largest cash crop in the United States.

GLOSSARY

Addictive Causing a physical or psychological need to use a habit-forming substance, such as drugs or alcohol.

Addiction Physical or psychological need to use drugs or alcohol.

Alveoli Small sacs in the lungs that are the gateway for gases and chemicals to enter the bloodstream.

Basal ganglia Part of the brain that controls unconscious muscle movements.

Cannabinoid Chemical found in the cannabis plant and in the brain.

Cannabinoid receptor Part of a neuron that processes cannabinoids.

Cannabis sativa Botanical name for marijuana.

Cash crop A plant grown and sold for profit, such as corn, cotton, or marijuana.

Cerebellum Part of the brain that helps to control coordination.

Gateway drug A drug whose use may lead to use of other, more dangerous drugs.

Hippocampus Area of the brain focused on short-term memory.

Hashish The pressed sap of the cannabis plant that can be smoked or eaten.

Hemp A cannabis plant used for its fibers.

Intoxicant A substance that causes users to feel "high" or "stoned."

Joint Marijuana cigarette.

Marijuana Anonymous (MA) An organization of former marijuana addicts that offers help to marijuana smokers who can't quit.

Neuron A brain cell.

Neurotransmitter A chemical that allows neurons to interact with each other.

Glossary

Plasma Liquid part of the blood.

Psychoactive Describing a chemical that causes changes in the brain.

THC Common term for delta-9-tetrahydrocannabinol, the psychoactive chemical in *Cannabis sativa*.

BIBLIOGRAPHY

Abel, Ernest. "Marijuana: The First Twelve Thousand Years." UK Cannabis Internet Activists. Available online. URL: http://www.ukcia.org/research/abel.htm. Accessed July 2, 2007.

Armentano, Paul. "Recent Research on Medical Marijuana." The National Organization for the Reform of Marijuana Laws. Available online. URL: http://www.norml.org/index.cfm?Group_ID=7002. Accessed July 2, 2007.

"Basic Facts About Drugs: Marijuana." American Council for Drug Education. Available online. URL: http://www.acde.org/common/Marijana.htm. Accessed July 2, 2007.

Bianco, Carl, M.D. "How Blood Works." Available online. URL: http://www.howstuffworks.com/blood.htm. Accessed July 2, 2007.

Bonsor, Kevin. "How Marijuana Works." Available online. URL: http://health.howstuffworks.com/marijuana1.htm. Accessed July 2, 2007.

Center on Addiction and Substance Abuse news release. "Cigarettes, Marijuana Linked for Teens." Available online. URL: http://alcoholism.about.com/cs/pot/a/blcasa030916.htm. Accessed July 2, 2007.

Cheng, Maria. "Marijuana May Increase Psychosis Risk." Associated Press. Available online: http://news.yahoo.com/s/ap/20070726/ap_on_he_me/marijuana_psychosis;_ylt=Am1tbTlAtrnxhfWOgLkZJJ0DW7oF

Ellickson, P.L., S.C. Martino, and R.L. Collins. "Marijuana use from adolescence to young adulthood: Multiple developmental trajectories and their associated outcomes." *Health Psychology* 23 no. 3 (2004): 299–307.

"Facts & Figures: Marijuana." U.S. Office of National Drug Control Policy. Available online. URL: http://www.whitehousedrugpolicy.gov/drugfact/marijuana/index.html. Accessed July 2, 2007.

Fergusson, D.M., L.J. Horwood, M.T. Lyndskey, and P.A.F. Madden. "Early reactions to cannabis predict later

Bibliography

dependence." *Archives of General Psychiatry* 60 no. 10 (2003): 1033–1039.

Freudenrich, Craig C., PhD. "How Your Brain Works." Available online. URL: http://www.howstuffworks.com/brain.htm. Accessed July 2, 2007.

Freuedenrich, Craig, C. "How Your Lungs Work." Available online. URL: http://www.howstuffworks.com/lung.htm. Accessed July 2, 2007.

Grim, Ryan. "A White House Drug Deal Gone Bad: Sitting on the negative results of a study of anti-marijuana ads." *Slate*, September 7, 2006. Available online. URL: http://www.slate.com/id/2148999/?nav=navoa. Accessed July 2, 2007.

Herning, Ronald. "Marijuana Use Affects Blood Flow In Brain Even After Abstinence." *Science Daily*, February 2005. Available online. URL: http://www.sciencedaily.com/releases/2005/02/050211084701.htm. Accessed July 2, 2007.

Hirschler, Ben. "Brain scans pinpoint cannabis mental health risk." Reuters News, April 30, 2007.

"History of Marijuana as Medicine: 2737 B.C. to Present." Medical Marijuana ProCon.org. Available online. URL: http://www.medicalmarijuanaprocon.org/pop/history.htm. Accessed July 2, 2007.

Hurley, Jennifer A., ed. *Addiction: Opposing Viewpoints*. San Diego, Calif.: Greenhaven Press, 2000.

"Initiation of Marijuana Use: Trends, Patterns, and Implications." U.S. Department of Health and Human Services, Office of Applied Studies. Available online. URL: http://www.oas.samhsa.gov/MJinitiation/highlights.htm. Accessed July 2, 2007.

"Inside the Teenage Brain." PBS Frontline. Available online. URL: http://www.pbs.org/wgbh/pages/frontline/shows/teenbrain. Accessed July 2, 2007.

Leshner, Dr. Alan I. "Top 10 Addiction Myths—and Myth Busters." Available online. URL: http://stories.silenttreatment.info/silent_03.asp.

Bibliography

Mears, Bill. "Supreme Court allows prosecution of medical marijuana." CNN.com, June 7, 2005. Available online. URL: http://www.cnn.com/2005/LAW/06/06/scotus.medical.marijuana. Accessed July 2, 2007.

National Commission on Marihuana and Drug Abuse. "History of Marihuana Use: Medical and Intoxicant." From *Marihuana, A Signal of Misunderstanding*, report of the U.S. National Commission on Marihuana and Drug Abuse, March 1972. Available online. URL: http://www.druglibrary.org/schaffer/Library/studies/nc/nc1a.htm. Accessed July 2, 2007.

"National Drug Threat Assessment 2007: Marijuana." National Drug Intelligence Center. Available online. URL: http://www.usdoj.gov/ndic/pubs21/21137/marijuana.htm. Accessed July 2, 2007.

"NIDA InfoFacts: Marijuana." National Institute on Drug Abuse. Available online. URL: http://www.nida.nih.gov/Infofacts/marijuana.html. Accessed July 2, 2007.

"Personal Stories of Marijuana Addicts." Marijuana Anonymous. Adapted from 1991 issues of *A New Leaf*, MA's newsletter. Available online. URL: http://www.marijuana-anonymous.org/Pages/stories.html. Accessed July 2, 2007.

"Twelve Questions." Marijuana Anonymous. URL: http://www.marijuana-anonymous.org/Pages/12quest.html. Accessed July 2, 2007.

Venkataraman, Nitya. "Marijuana Called Top U.S. Cash Crop." ABCNews.com, December 2006. Available online. URL: http://abcnews.go.com/Business/story?id=2735017. Accessed July 2, 2007.

Whitebread, Charles. "The History of the Non-Medical Use of Drugs in the United States." Schaffer Library of Drug Policy. Available online. URL: http://www.druglibrary.org/schaffer/History/whiteb1.htm. Accessed July 2, 2007.

Williams-Schlabig, Jill. "Cognitive Deficits in Marijuana Smokers Persist After Use Stops." NIDA Notes, September

Bibliography

2006. Available online. URL: http://www.nida.nih.gov/NIDA_Notes/NNVol18N5/Cognitive.html. Accessed July 2, 2007.

"Worried First-Time Marijuana Smoker." Teen Health FX, July 2002. Available online. URL: http://www.teenhealthfx.com/answers/Alcohol/47.html. Accessed July 2, 2007.

FURTHER READING

Bingham, Jane. *Marijuana: What's the Deal?* Portsmouth, N.H.: Heinemann, 2005.

Connolly, Sean. *Marijuana: Straight Talking*. Los Angeles: Smart Apple Publishers, 2006.

Goodwin, William. *Drug Education Library: Marijuana*. San Diego: Lucent Press, 2002.

Lennard-Brown, Sarah. *Marijuana*. Health Issues. Chicago: Raintree, 2004.

NIH Editors. *Marijuana, Facts for Teens*. Bethesda, Md.: National Institutes of Health, 2004.

Ruschman, Paul. *Legalizing Marijuana*. Point/Counterpoint. New York: Chelsea House, 2003.

Tardiff, Joe. *Marijuana*. Contemporary Issues. San Diego: Greenhaven Press, 2007.

WEB SITES

THE TEEN BRAIN IS A WORK IN PROGRESS
http://www.pbs.org/wgbh/pages/frontline/shows/teenbrain/work

The Internet home of PBS's *Frontline* presents information on the growth and development of the teenage brain.

MARIJUANA ANONYMOUS
http://www.marijuana-anonymous.org/index.shtml

The Web site of this organization for marijuana addicts provides information on treatment and how to reach out for help.

MARIJUANA AND MENTAL HEALTH
http://www.theantidrug.com/drug_info/marijuana_mental_health.asp

This site contains a lot of information about the affect of marijuana on adolescents, as well as tips for staying away from the drug.

Further Reading

NIDA INFOFACTS

http://www.nida.nih.gov/Infofacts/marijuana.html

Read more on survey results about marijuana use among young people.

SHAFFER LIBRARY OF DRUG POLICY

http://www.druglibrary.org/schaffer

Browse through an encyclopedia of information about marijuana and other drugs.

PHOTO CREDITS

PAGE

13: Getty Images
15: Ben Smith/www.shutterstock.com
17: Pascal Goetgheluck/Photo Researchers Inc.
20: AP Images
22: AP Images
31: © Lee Snider/Photo Images/CORBIS
35: HIP/Art Resource
38: Vanni/Art Resource, NY
40: The Granger Collection, New York
42: Scala/Art Resource
44: Courtesy of The Library of Congress LC-USZ62-41172
51: AP Images
58: © Infobase Publishing
61: Pablo Paul/Alamy
62: Getty Images
66: © Infobase Publishing
67: Getty Images
76: Time & Life Pictures/Getty Images
84: AP Images
85: AP Images

COVER

©Vova Pomortzeff/ Shutterstock.com

INDEX

A

addiction
   determining, 88–89
   as disease, 87
   family background and, 32
   getting help for, 89–90
   joking about, 82
   outcomes of, 82–87
   psychological, 78–80, 82
addictive drugs, 12–14
adults, trends in marijuana use among, 29–32
advertisements, 29
age of exploration, 41–42
alveoli, 57, 59
American Medical Association (AMA), 79
American Revolution, 45
Anslinger, Harry, 50–54
anti-marijuana laws, 49, 54–55
appearance, 91
appetite, 71, 72
average marijuana user, 22–23
avoiding marijuana, 92–93

B

baby boomers, 21
basal ganglia, 65, 66
beliefs, personal, 92
bhang, 37–39
blood, 63
body, effects of marijuana on
   overview, 56–57
   brain, 32–33, 64–66, 76–78
   circulatory system, 63–64
   eating marijuana and, 62–63
   lungs, how they work, 57–58
   lungs and marijuana, 58–61
   medical use and, 67–68
bongs, 14
brain, effects of marijuana on, 32–33, 64–66, 76–78. *See also* mind, effects of marijuana on
breathing, 57, 59, 64
bronchioles, 59

C

California, 46
cancer, 60–61, 68
cannabinoid receptors
   appetite and, 71
   brain development and, 78
   defined, 65
   long-term effects, 73
   psychoactive effects and, 70
cannabinoids, 16–18, 19, 57. *See also* THC (tetrahydrocannabinol)
Cannabis sativa, 14
canvas, 19
carbon dioxide, 57–58
cash crops, 22–23
cell and connection growth in the brain, 76–77
cerebellum, 65, 66, 78
China, 34–37
chronic relapsing, 87
cigarette smoking, 32, 59–61
circulatory system, 63–64
cloth from hemp, 19, 41
clothes made of hemp, 36
colonial North America, 43–45
communists, 50–54
concentration, 75
Cortes, Hernando, 45
cotton, 47–48
coughing, 59
cutting away, 77
cutting back, 76

D

damage to lungs, 60
depression, 73
digestion, 62–63
Disocorides, 39
drug hunger, 80
drug testing, 83, 85–86
DrugScience.org, 22–23
D'Souza, Deepak Cyril, 74
dumb things, doing, 91

Index

E
eating marijuana, 18, 62–63
effects of marijuana. *See* body, effects of marijuana on; brain, effects of marijuana on; mind, effects of marijuana on
Egypt, 47
Europe, 39–41, 46–47
European exploration, 41–43

F
family background, 32
floating feeling, 71
friends using marijuana, 90–92

G
Galen, 41
gateway drugs, 32, 79
Giedd, Jay, 77
Great Depression, 50
Greece, 39

H
hair test, 86
harmful, perception of marijuana as, 28
hashish, 14, 47
"health tonics," 48
heart, 64
"heavy users," 78
help and treatment
  overview, 81–82
  addiction and, 82–87
  avoiding marijuana, 92–93
  friends using marijuana, 90–92
  testing, 85–86
  treatment for addiction, 87–90
hemp, 19–20, 36, 41–48
Henry VIII, 43
Herodotus, 39
highs, 57, 72
hippocampus, 65, 77
history of cannabis, hemp, and marijuana
  19th-century America, 47–48
  American Revolution, 45
  ancient China, 34–37
  ancient India, 37–39
  English colonies, 43–44
  European Exploration and, 41–43
  from hemp to marijuana in early 20th century, 48–50
  as intoxicant, 37, 46–47
  Spanish Empire, 45–46
  spread to youth after World War II, 50–55
  westward movement to Europe, 39–41
hunger, 71, 72. *See also* drug hunger
hypothalamus, 71

I
immuno-assay test, 86
India, 37–39
Institute of Medicine (IOM), 68
intoxicant, cannabis as, 34, 37, 46–47
Islam, 47

J
Jamestown, Virginia, 43
Jefferson, Thomas, 45
joints, 61

L
laws against marijuana, 48–49, 54–55
legalization of marijuana, 52–53
"light users," 78
liver, 63–64
lung cancer, 60–61
lungs, 57–61

Index

M
Marihuana Tax Act, 50
Marijuana Anonymous (MA), 88–89, 90
"marijuana," origins of term, 49
Marijuana Potency Project, 16
Marinol, 68
medical marijuana use
  overview, 18
  in ancient China, 36–37
  effects on the body, 67–68
  "health tonics," 48
  regulation of, 48–49
Medical Research Institute of New Zealand, 60
memory, 75, 91
mental problems, 73–75
metabolites, 86
Mexican immigrants, 49–50
Mexican revolution, 49
Mexico, 46
Middle Ages, 41, 46
Middle East, 47
mind, effects of marijuana on. *See also* brain, effects of marijuana on
  overview, 69–70
  brain development and, 76–78
  damage and costs, 72–76
  gateway drugs and, 79
  psychoactive effects, 70–72
  psychological addiction, 78–80
money, hemp used for, 45
munchies, 71
music, 92

N
names for marijuana, 14
National Drug Control Policy Office, 26, 53
National Football League (NFL), 83
National Household Survey on Drug Abuse, 73
National Institute on Drug Abuse (NIDA), 22, 25–29, 33, 79
National Institutes of Health (NIH), 12, 25
negative activities, 77
neurons, 65
neurotransmitters, 65
New England, 43–44
New Spain, 46
New York Times, 49
nicknames for marijuana, 14
NIDA surveys, 25–29, 33. *See also* National Institute on Drug Abuse (NIDA)
"no," how to say, 93

O
Ohio Medicine Society, 48
oxygen, 57

P
papermaking, 19, 36
perception of "great risk," 28
personal beliefs, 92
pipes, 14
plasma, 63
platelets, 63
positive activities, 77
prohibition, 49
promises, 87
psychoactive effects, 70–72
psychological addiction, 78–80, 82
psychotic disorders, 74
pulmonary system, 64
Pure Food and Drug Act, 48–49

R
reasons for saying no to marijuana, 30–31
reasons for using marijuana, 18

Index

receptors, 65
red blood cells, 63
relapsing, chronic, 87
relaxing without drugs, 91–92
Revolutionary War, American, 45
risky choice, smoking marijuana as, 25
Rolfe, John, 43
Roman Empire, 39–41
rope made of hemp, 41, 47–48

S

sails, 47
San Jose, California, 46
schizophrenia, 74, 75
Scythians, 39
Shafer Commission, 78–79
short-term memory, 75, 91
Shovelton, Helena, 61
sinsemilla, 16
Siva (Hindu god), 37
slavery, 48
smoking marijuana, 17, 58–61
Spanish Empire, 45–46
sports for relaxing, 91–92
spread of marijuana use in U.S., 18–21, 50–55
steel, 48
stomach, 62
stoned state, 72, 73
suicidal thoughts, 73–75
summertime drug abuse, 26
supervision by adults, 26
surveys, NIDA, 25–29

T

Taiwan, 34–35
teenagers, trends in marijuana use among, 25–29
testing for marijuana use, 83, 85–86
THC (tetrahydrocannabinol)
  overview, 16–18
  brain and, 64, 65
  drug testing and, 85–86
  high from, 57
  in liver, 64
  long-term effects, 73
  lungs and, 59
  in Marinol pills, 68
  psychoactive effects, 70–72
throat irritation, 60
tobacco, 32, 43, 59–61
tolerance, 73
treatment. *See* help and treatment

V

Vedas, 39
Vikings, 41
Virginia, 43, 45, 54
Volkow, Nora, 26, 28

W

Washington, George, 45
weight, 71
wheezing, 59
white blood cells, 63
White House Office of National Drug Control Policy, 26, 53
Whitebread, Charles, 18–20
Williams, Ricky, 83–87
withdrawal, 89–90
work and marijuana, 75–76

Z

Zammit, Stanley, 74

ABOUT THE AUTHORS

W. SCOTT INGRAM is the author of more than 50 books for young people. He is the recipient of six Educational Press awards for his writing, including the 1999 Fiction Award for his short story "Shadowland." In 2005, Ingram received an NAACP Image Award for Children's Literature for his book *The 1963 Civil Rights March*. He is a graduate of the University of Connecticut, and now lives in Portland, Connecticut.

Series introduction author **RONALD J. BROGAN** is the Bureau Chief for the New York City office of D.A.R.E. (Drug Abuse Resistance Education) America, where he trains and coordinates more than 100 New York City police officers in program-related activities. He also serves as a D.A.R.E. regional director for Oregon, Connecticut, Massachusetts, Maine, New Hampshire, New York, Rhode Island, and Vermont. In 1997, Brogan retired from the U.S. Drug Enforcement Administration (DEA), where he served as a special agent for 26 years. He holds bachelor's and master's degrees in criminal justice from the City University of New York.